Blow: Three Little Pigs Retold

DEMELZA CARLTON

A tale in the Romance a Medieval Fairy Tale series

This is a work of fiction. Names, characters, businesses, places, events and incidents are either the products of the author's imagination or used in a fictitious manner. Any resemblance to actual persons, living or dead, or actual events is purely coincidental.

Copyright © 2017 Demelza Carlton

Lost Plot Press

All rights reserved.

ISBN-13: 978-0-9922693-1-9

ISBN-10: 0-9922693-1-8

DEDICATION

This book is dedicated to my husband. For who knew some Polish moonshine, followed by a week-long whisky tour would result in something like this?

One

Midsummer festival fever had caught them all in her heathen coils. The higher born boys fought with practice swords in the yard, their bouts descending into pitched battle with no guard or master at arms to break it up. Rudolf found himself stunned in the dust, unnoticed by the others as they pursued longer held grudges against boys they knew, and he scrambled to his feet. Retreating from the yard seemed the most chivalrous thing to do, for he had more training than most of them, though not enough to stop the fight like his cousin Reidar might have.

Outside the walls, pine had been piled up for the bonfires, huge as haystacks, that would be set alight after dark to feed some ancient, beastly god. Now, the fresh, life-giving scent of the pine lay sharp over the bed of long-dead peat from the bogs, reminding him of the inevitability of death, even in the bright summer sun.

His thick furs itched in the unaccustomed heat that was so little like home, but he did not dare take them off. They marked him for what he was, a Viken prince among these Islanders, who wore linen and leather that was surely more suitable for summer.

Peat smoke spiralled in a dark prayer to heaven as it roasted pork to what he hoped would be perfection. The rich smell took him back home, to his farewell feast and the roasted beast that had been Reidar's first kill. Oh, now that had been a feast. Could these foreigners match it?

The crack of what sounded like a spitting

cat forced his eyes open. No, it was just the beast's flesh spitting at the coals that roasted it, like its last act of courage before the old gods took it to Valhalla. Did pigs go to heaven, though, he wondered. The men of the new faith said no, but he didn't know enough about the old to be sure.

Hogs probably went up to the great feasting table in the sky, much like their bodies had here. Such was their fate, as this exile was his. At least he was not a pig, however much he roasted in his northern clothes.

He headed away from the clamour, toward the cliffs.

"Boy, boy!" an imperious, elderly voice called.

Rudolf turned. He'd learned the hard way not to ignore an old woman's commands. If he hadn't sat on that throne for a moment and Queen Regina hadn't caught him, then he wouldn't be here, exiled at the other end of the world. Better alive than dead, though, and alive, he could train more so that one day, he could better serve his king. The man whose backside belonged on that cursed throne.

If the approaching woman was Queen Regina, Rudolf would have run. As it was, he forced himself to hold his ground.

The woman everyone called Nurse limped up to him. "Have you seen them? Wee devils, they are. Their father insists they must attend the feast dressed in their best, and I cannot find them anywhere!"

The Lord Angus's daughters were missing? Rudolf's heart turned to ice, as he remembered the day he'd lost his little sister to the ice on the fjords.

But there was no ice here, and little water, either, for the burns that had flowed only yesterday were little more than mud now after days without rain. It truly was a different world to Viken.

If he had a choice, today he would be in the swimming hole the other boys had spoken of. A pool they said never dried up.

A place deep enough for a little girl to drown.

Panic gave his feet wings as he crested the rise, following the dried up burn. If he could get there in time, perhaps he could save them.

Perhaps…

A shrill scream stopped his heart, but not his feet. Still he ran. If a girl could scream, she could breathe, and he could still save her. By all the saints in heaven, please let him save her.

Low hanging branches sliced at his face, but still Rudolf ran on until he almost fell over the lip of the pool, or what had been the pool. Perhaps even this morning, it had still held water, but now…now it held three wriggling, shrieking girls as they played in liquid mud. Alive. Safe. All three. Portia, Lina and Arlie, so covered in mud he couldn't tell them apart – not that it was an easy matter anyway, given the girls looked identical.

Rudolf's heart dared to beat again and he took a deep breath. "Nurse!" he shouted. "I have found your three little pigs!"

Two

"You fought well today, and you have a knack for commanding men. I know several men owe you their lives after today, for it was your quick thinking in the heat of battle that saved them."

Rudolf's chest puffed at Angus's praise.

Angus continued, "You'll need new armour soon. You're not a boy any more, and your shoulders are too wide for that breastplate. Where there's gaps, an arrow will find them," Angus said, throwing the reins of his horse to a groom.

Rudolf did the same, but he lingered to stroke Hector's side as he was led off. He'd never owned a finer horse. Not back in Viken, or since he arrived here. How many years had it been now? At least six. Maybe seven.

"You like him, don't you? See, I told Lewis he couldn't sell him off the islands. Valuable breeding stock, he'll be, when you're not riding him."

Rudolf remembered his manners. "Thank you again, Lord Angus. He's a princely gift indeed."

Angus waved away his thanks. "No more than you deserve. My own father gave me my first warhorse when I reached manhood. My first ride, the bastard reared up and threw me on my arse. My brother laughed himself sick. You have a much better seat than did at your age. Better than Portia, though better not tell her I said that."

Rudolf laughed. "No, I won't, as long as you know that's what I'll be thinking about when I'm staring at her bottom next time we go riding."

"Man your age should be looking for a wife.

I know I was. Or will your father be sending one from Viken?"

Viken? Why would he send a girl after him? This was home. Rudolf would likely never see Viken again. "Viken girls choose their husbands, just like the ones here," Rudolf managed to say. "I left no sweetheart behind me, so no girl will be coming to find me."

An explosion of red blasted through the door to the longhouse. "There they are! I found them," Portia cried, tossing her hair off her face. She'd forgotten her shoes again, and with no Nurse to remind her any more, she'd probably been wearing holes in her stockings the whole time they'd been away.

"I brought you a gift," Rudolf said, pulling the feather from under his breastplate. He'd kept it in the pocket over his heart. "At the end of the battle, when those rank cowards were running away, a golden eagle circled the field and dropped it. Landed right at my feet. I thought you might like a new quill."

Portia dashed up to him and plucked the feather from his hand. Then she threw her arms around him and hugged him. Rudolf laughed as he returned her hug, conscious of Angus's thoughtful eyes on him.

Angus was planning something, to be sure.

"Can we go riding now?" Portia demanded. The woman-child had all the impatience of a child, while her body grew more and more into a woman's form.

Rudolf laughed again. "I have been riding all day, and Hector, too. I am starving. I hope you have a good dinner ordered."

Portia would not be put off. "Tomorrow, then? If we leave early, we might be able to make it up to Loch Findlugan, and search for its secret. While you were away, I went through Mother's things and found a scroll about the history of Isla. It said the standing stones – "

Angus interrupted, "Tomorrow, Rudolf needs to be measured for new armour. He's outgrown his."

Portia laughed. "Must be all the food he eats. And people call me and my sisters pigs!" This earned Rudolf a glare.

Rudolf hung his head. The tale of him finding the three little sisters, wallowing in the mud like pigs, had spread rapidly through the Southern Isles, as all good stories did. Even if seven years had passed since that day, Portia still had not forgiven him. She might never.

He glanced at Angus. "I'm sure I won't be needed all day for new armour. There will be time for a ride tomorrow. Perhaps not to Loch Findlugan, but we can take the horses for a ride on the beach."

Portia enveloped him in another hug, tighter and longer than the first. "I love you, Dolf!"

Rudolf patted her back awkwardly, his eyes offering an apology to Angus.

Angus nodded, unconcerned. "Enough talk of tomorrow. I'm famished. I fancy a fine leg of mutton for dinner, and I'm sure Rudolf does, too. Release your prisoner, Portia." He headed inside.

Portia let go, then tucked her hand into Rudolf's. "I'll release you on one condition. You must tell me all about the battle over dinner. How many men you killed, whether you were close enough to hear their last words…or did you shoot them with your bow?"

She was the same age as he'd been when he arrived on Isla, Rudolf realised, and just as bloodthirsty. "I did not use my bow this time. Angus had archers enough."

"I want my own bow. Viken women sometimes go to war with their men, you said. I could be one of the archers and kill those cowardly, thieving Albans before they could step ashore!"

Rudolf laughed. "Are you strong enough to draw a bow yet?"

Portia pouted. "No."

"When you are full grown, like me, you may practice with mine. If you can hit the target, I promise you I will see that you have your own bow."

Her eyes lit with the fire that seemed to burn without cease within her. "Really?"

Rudolf could refuse her nothing. He prayed that Angus would agree. "Really."

Three

Portia reacted to the king's demands the way she always did when something vexed her: she went shooting.

Her bow was a comforting weight in her hand as she marched to the practice field. The smooth wood was exactly the right size for someone of her stature – as Rudolf must have known, for he'd given it to her on her last name day. Much easier to shoot with than his own monster bow, easily taller than he was. It had taken her years before she'd had the strength to fire anything from his bow, but when a lucky shot clipped the target, Rudolf had made good on his promise – a bow of her own, and archery lessons to keep her from shooting him instead of the target.

Not that she'd meant to do that. The arrow had accidentally gone through his boot, and she'd told him so. She wasn't sure he believed her, though. She sighed and took aim.

She emptied her quiver in record speed, wishing the plain wood target had a picture of the king's face painted on it. She did not even know what the bastard looked like. She imagined King Donald as old and fat with thinning hair, a petulant fool who demanded things that were not his like the spoiled child he'd once been.

She fitted an arrow to the bowstring.

How dare he try to claim her lands. Her father's lands, truly, but hers, too, for she was his firstborn.

She drew the arrow back.

How dare he insist they pay him tribute. A man who had no right to their lands, or the fruit from it.

She sighted along the arrow, blowing out

her breath in a rush.

How dare he call their people foreigners. How dare he!

She released, and the arrow flew toward the target. It lodged in the side, so close to the edge that it only hung there for a moment before it fell to earth.

Earth that sorry excuse for a king had no claim on!

Portia stomped her foot for emphasis.

"Looking at the target, I wondered if Arlie had picked up a bow for her annual archery practice. But Arlie doesn't stamp her foot like that." Rudolf gestured at the target across the field. "Are you feeling sorry for the target, Portia? Trying not to hit it because hitting it would be cruel?"

Portia's face turned as red as her hair. Trust Rudolf to bring that up. No one else remembered something that happened ten years ago, except him. "I still think butchering pigs is cruel, but nothing I can say or do will stop it, for the rest of your will still eat it. So will I, and be properly thankful to the animal that gave its life so that we may eat its flesh."

She sounded like the priest at last Sunday's mass, and she knew it. Before Rudolf could tease her for that, too, she continued, "It won't matter if I miss my target, anyway. Men all bunch up in an army, so if I miss one man, I'm bound to hit the one beside him."

He laughed. "Since when are you riding to war? Your father is not so short of men he'll need you to fight." His gaze travelled from her feet up to her face. "Unless you plan on wearing a man's garb. There's many a man on the island who's dreamed of seeing you without your gown, but I'm sure none of them imagined you'd be wearing armour."

Just as her blush faded, it flamed into life once more. Only Rudolf could say these things with such brutal honesty, without apology. Not for the first time, she wondered if he'd been one of those dreaming men. Men who would soon be off to war, with no time to dream of anyone, she told herself sternly. "I have no need to ride to war. Raiders come in boats when they see fit, and if the menfolk are not at home, then it falls to us women to defend our homes."

Rudolf inclined his head. "So it does. Here in the south, right up to Viken in the north. But your father will never leave you here unprotected, and you will always have me." He drew a dagger from his belt and sent it flying toward the target. He hit the centre. "I will defend you with my life, Portia."

That serious look in his eyes heated her all over again, but not just her face this time. There was something about Rudolf that lit a fire inside her. The kind of fire she liked, but could never stoke. "I'm sure my father will be very grateful for your service," she said sweetly.

He opened his mouth, but no words came out. Then he shook his head, as if to rid it of ideas that had no place there, a feeling Portia understood well. Finally, he said, "But it would be lax of me to stop you from practising, when you so sorely need it."

"Why you – " Portia began, then stopped as Rudolf grinned. When he smiled, the man was charming enough to coax a honeycomb from an angry bear. Not even she was immune to him. Perhaps that's why she felt so hot inside.

"Help me retrieve my arrows, then."

Rudolf pulled the lucky few from the target while she hunted through the grass for the rest. When the quiver was more than half full once more, she marched back to where she'd left her bow. Rudolf with his longer strides got there first, lifting the weapon in readiness, though he didn't hand it to her.

"First, I must check your stance, Portia," he said. "Show me how you stand."

Never one to like being ordered about, Portia set her hand on her hip and waved an arrow. "You'd better hope I don't decide to make you my target instead."

"You wouldn't do that," he said easily. "You like me."

No matter how much he irritated her and make her feel other unwelcome feelings she had to ruthlessly suppress, Portia had to admit she did. Not aloud, though. "I might also like to see you hopping around with an arrow in your foot again."

"You have your dreams and I have mine. I like mine better. Now, do you wish to practise, or no?"

Portia relented and stepped up to the bow, angling herself so that she faced Rudolf and not the target. She fitted her arrow to the string. "There. Good enough for you?"

Rudolf inspected her, even going as far as to march right the way around her, before he nudged her foot with his. "Your stance needs to be a little wider, pointed to where you wish the arrow to go." His arms came around her, lifting the bow so that the arrow no longer pointed at the ground.

Portia wanted to relax into his embrace, and surrender to the promise of protection he offered. It would be so easy, and yet it was something she could never do. Rudolf was a foreigner, a ward sent from Viken to learn to fight in her father's house. One day, he would be summoned home to fight for whatever Viken lord his family owed fealty to. Portia was her father's eldest daughter, and heir to Isla. The man she married would follow her father as Lord of Isla, the largest and most powerful of the Southern Isles. She could never marry a mere household knight. It would take a lord at least, or a lord's son, to hold

Father's place in council. Rudolf knew this as well as she did, which was why he never took liberties, though he made it very clear he would like to. But that was an invitation she could never offer.

She straightened, paying more attention to the bow and arrow than the boy whose breath tickled the back of her neck. "Which foot do you like best, Dolf?" she asked.

"Your left one, because that's pointed at the target," he said, cupping her elbow in his hand. "Now draw, sight along the arrow..." His hand slammed into her gut, just below her breasts, forcing her to exhale. "Now I've made you breathless, you may shoot."

The arrow whistled across the field and thwacked into the target. Not in the centre, marked by the divot from Rudolf's knife, but nearer than any of her earlier attempts.

"There!"

Rudolf inclined his head. "Not bad. If you were aiming for a man's heart, you might have hit him in the throat. But we can improve on that."

With infinite patience Portia knew she

would never possess, Rudolf helped her empty her quiver – all into the target this time. Then he headed across the field with her to retrieve the arrows again.

When the quiver was full, he held it out and asked, "Are you still angry, or have you done enough shooting for one day?"

Until she hit the centre of the target every time, it would not be enough. She sighed. A landless knight like Rudolf would not understand. "One more time," she said, reaching for the quiver.

Rudolf caught her hand in his. "You're bleeding. I say you have done enough. We should get you inside, so one of your sisters can bandage these fingers. You can practise more on the morrow, but first, I must get you some pigs' ears."

"Pigs' ears are no use to anyone, except the pig itself," Portia said, snatching her hand back. Her fingers tingled where he'd touched them, a hint of magic that called for more. She refused to yield. Isla would not yield.

Rudolf chuckled. "Get you to your sisters. I'll return your things to the armoury, and find you inside." He shouldered both her quiver and her bow and headed across the yard.

Portia sucked on her bleeding fingers as she headed inside. Arlie would exclaim over the blood, fanning herself in case she fainted. Lina would be the one to clean and bandage her, like Nurse had taught her to before age and infirmity had called the old woman from this life.

As it would one day call them all.

But not yet, if Portia had any say in it.

Four

The moment Arlie spotted Rudolf, she cried, "Dolf will go to war to save us! Won't you, Dolf?"

Portia hushed her. She might only be a few minutes older than her sisters, but sometimes the difference felt like years.

"If you ladies need saving, I would be honoured to be of service," Rudolf said as he approached. He met Portia's eyes without a hint of laughter and bowed low. "From what must I save you? Is there another spider?"

Lina laughed. "No, only Portia screams at

spiders. This time, it's some pompous king, demanding tribute from all the island lords, which they will not pay."

"That's no way to talk about your liege," Rudolf said mildly. "I've never heard anyone call King Harald pompous before."

"That's because it's not him!" Arlie giggled. "It's some silly foreigner called Donald. He calls for tithes and men, to combat what he calls our foreign invaders, so that he might help us make the Southern Isles great again."

"Nay, he wants to make Alba great again, but he insists we are an important part of it," Lina corrected.

Portia frowned. "Important enough to attract his interest, because he thinks we might offer him men or money. No king has every offered us anything we didn't have to pay for. Not King Harald or this Donald. The lords of the isles know this, and they will refuse him, which will mean war."

"The lords are in the right of it. The isles are under Harald's protection, and they do not belong to some man called Donald. If he wants them, he will have to fight for them, and pay dearly," Rudolf declared.

Now Portia thought of it, he did sound like one of the lords. Somehow, over the years, Rudolf the boy had turned into a man, or at least something like one. A pity he would never be one of them. Because if he was...

"Perhaps this Donald should just ask to marry Portia. We all know no man on the islands is good enough for her, for she turns her nose up at all of them. Would a king suit you, Portia?" Arlie teased.

Rudolf's eyes were upon her, and Portia found she could not meet them. "Father knows as well as I do that I can only wed a man who can hold the islands. Hold them, and defend them, like he has. All this Donald has done is blow wind at us, and the isles have withstood greater gales than anything he's thrown at us thus far. I will wed when a strong enough man presents himself, and not before."

"See? Portia will never marry for love. Or she'd have picked Rudolf, long ago," Lina declared with a smile.

Arlie dissolved in a fit of giggles, falling back to kick her legs in the air.

Once again, Portia felt far too hot. She rose and marched out of the room, the sound of her sisters' laughter following her. And booted footsteps. Rudolf, of course.

"Portia," he began cautiously, as if wishing to warn her of his presence.

She turned and held up her hand to halt him before he said any more. "My sisters like to joke at my expense. And yours. I'm sorry if their levity sounds insulting to your ears. You are a strong and skilled warrior. Both my father and I know that. So do my sisters, I think. But when we hear whispered news of war…well, you see how we react. Lina will pick herbs to dry for every wound and ailment imaginable, and fill the cellars with all the food she can possibly preserve. Arlie…she will make light of everything, as she always does, for laughter is her way."

"And you shall shoot things, because even if every man on this island dies in battle, you will still defend it while you have breath left in your body," Rudolf finished for her. "Isla is your home, and the Southern Isles are your kingdom as much as Harald holds Viken, or

Donald does Alba."

Now it was Portia's turn to laugh. "No one understands me the way you do, Dolf. I swear it is as though you have some magical power to see into my head. I'm glad I didn't shoot you."

Rudolf laughed with her. "I'm glad you didn't shoot me, either. If it comes to war, I hope I am never on the opposing side to you and your father. I meant it when I said I would protect you." He held out his hand. "Here."

Portia glanced down and recoiled. "What in heaven's name do you intend to do with those?"

"Give me your hand."

Reluctantly, she did as he asked. He wrapped the pig's ear around her middle finger, the leather surprisingly warm and soft from being in his pocket. Next, he threaded a thin leather thong through the holes edging the ear, until he'd laced it like one of her gowns. He pulled the whole thing taut, then tied it at the bottom. "Now the others." Soon he'd shrouded all three of her middle fingers in pigs' ears. The leather was paler than boot leather, as though the pigs' ears were tanned differently. In fact, the pigskin was so close to the shade of her own skin that it looked like she wasn't wearing the finger guards at all. "Next time, wear these when you need to shoot out your frustration. Your arms will tire long before you make your fingers bleed. Pigs' ears are tough."

"Thank you, Dolf!" Portia threw her arms around his neck. Too late, she realised as her body moulded to his that she shouldn't do such things any more. Though he cared for her as much as any brother, Rudolf was most certainly not one of her siblings. Awkwardly, she peeled herself away from him, only now realising that he held his arms stiffly at his sides. Stopping himself from returning her embrace, or pushing her away? Oh, she was so stupid.

"It's my pleasure, Portia," he said. With a slight bow, he left her.

Portia sighed, only now realising she held her well-wrapped fingers over her heart. If only she was as free as her sisters. But the world didn't work the way she wanted to, for life was nothing like a fairytale.

Five

When Angus, Lord of Isla, slumped into his seat at dinner, no one dared ask what made him so weary, for they all knew. Lina gestured imperiously for servants to fill her father's plate, while Portia poured wine for him. He would share what he knew after dinner, and not before.

It wasn't until Angus dismissed the servants that Rudolf began to worry about what he might say. If he wanted to share secrets with his family alone, then Rudolf should retire and save the man from doing him the dishonour of dismissing him.

Rudolf rose. "I took Hector for a long ride today, and it occurs to me that he was limping a little toward the end. I should go check on him before it gets too dark to see."

Angus lifted his hand. "Stay, Rudolf. What I have to say concerns you, too. The horse can wait until morning."

Rudolf sat down. He could feel Portia's curious gaze upon him, but he forced himself to keep his own eyes on Lord Angus. Hope flared in his breast, but he forced it back behind his ribs.

Angus drained his cup and set it down with finality. "As you all know, King Donald of Alba has laid claim to the islands, and a list of the tribute that he believes is his due. Tribute we have failed to pay in the past, he says, which must be paid, too. He sent these demands by way of a messenger, who was commanded to read Donald's missive aloud to me, and all the other lords, to make sure we understood. For, apparently, we are an illiterate lot on the Southern Isles, or so he says."

This time, it was Lina who leaped to her

feet. "I suggest all the lords should pen him a message by their own hands, suggesting he shove his missive up his arse. No, that he instruct his messenger to do it for him, as he probably can't find his arse with both hands and a map." As quickly as she'd risen, she subsided again. Lina was both as calm and relentless as the sea. She'd make some man a good wife, one day, as long as he let her run his household without interfering.

Angus waved a hand in acknowledgement. "Our response to Donald is something all the lords of the isles will decide in council. I sent my own messenger with his, so they should start arriving soon, and I will be there to greet them when they do." He turned thoughtful eyes toward Rudolf. "I'd like you to come with me."

"So shall I!" Portia declared.

"No. You must stay here and protect your sisters," Angus said. "This may be a council of war, and no place for you. Your presence would complicate matters." He deliberately didn't look at her.

Portia looked ready to explode.

Rudolf placed a sympathetic hand on her wrist. "I would be honoured to attend a council. Then I will be able to carry a full account of the decisions back to the girls here if you are called away by other responsibilities."

Portia yanked her arm away. "You'd better," she said darkly.

She said little to him for the rest of the meal, and for the days before Rudolf departed with her father for Loch Findlugan. Her father received a fond farewell, but Rudolf merely earned a pointed look before she disappeared into the practice yard, where the thwack of arrows hitting the target could soon be heard.

He and Angus were barely out of sight along the road before the lord asked, "What do you think of her?"

"I think Portia is a lovely, strong-minded young woman," Rudolf said cautiously.

Angus laughed. "The stubbornest of my three little pigs, you mean. If it comes to war, as I fear it might, she would take up a sword to fight right alongside the rest of us. It would have been better for her if she'd been born a boy."

"I would not like her so much if she was," Rudolf said without thinking. He regretted the words the moment they left his lips, but it was too late to retrieve them.

Angus turned an appraising eye in his direction. "Yes, and she likes you, too. She doesn't think anyone notices, but sometimes she looks at you the way her mother used to regard me. She listens to you, too, though she won't listen to anyone else. Maybe you'll be able to control her."

Rudolf burst out laughing. "Control Portia? I pity the man who tries. She will huff and puff and blow his manhood away. She is your daughter, after all."

"And as my daughter, she is also my heir, as I'm sure you know." Angus paused, as if he wanted this to sink in. Finally, he continued, "The man who marries her will also inherit her claim to Isla, when I am gone, and perhaps even my place in council, if the other lords accept him. Birthright is not enough here on the Southern Isles, you understand. A man must also be a leader and a warrior worth following."

Rudolf nodded. His father had told him the same thing when he was a boy in Viken. Varg was the older brother, yet Harald had become king. "My people are much the same. This way, if a king dies while his sons are still young, another man may take the throne while the sons are brought up like any other highborn warriors. When the next king dies…his successor is chosen from among the men with suitable claims of birth, blood and marriage, but he must have the strength to lead the…I suppose you would call them chieftains, much like your lords."

"Here on the islands, every lord is a king within his borders, for an ocean separates him from the others. We have no kings."

This was less true than it appeared, as Rudolf well knew. "Ah, but there is King Harald, whose claim to these lands is responsible for the kind hospitality you have offered me for so many years. And this King Donald, a neighbour who covets what isn't his. And there is yourself, a lord among lords. If the islands had their own king, it would be you."

Angus nodded in satisfaction, as though this was the answer he'd hoped for. "You've fought with us, as one of us."

"We both serve the same king. Protecting these lands is as much my responsibility as it is yours, though I do not command any men." Yet, Rudolf added silently. He'd distinguished himself in the battles and raiding parties he had fought in, to the point where he easily assumed command when circumstances required it. Lord Angus had taught him battle tactics and strategy were just as important as the strength of his army when battle was joined. But the men he commanded had always belonged to Lord Angus.

Unlike his father, who commanded all the armies of Viken, and the ships, too.

Lord Angus seemed to read his thoughts. "You fight well in the field, and the men follow you. That is no small thing in a land like this one. You understand battle tactics better than most, both on and off the field."

Rudolf was not accustomed to such high praise. "It is a while since I have had a worthy opponent. Perhaps you would agree to a chess match while we wait for the other lords to arrive?" He patted his saddle bag. "I brought mine."

Lord Angus shook his head. "I think your skills at that game surpassed mine a long time ago. But never let it be said that I turned down an offer for battle. We shall play on the shores of Loch Findlugan after the sun sets."

"I look forward to it."

They rode on in silence, lost in their own separate thoughts. As they always did, Rudolf's thoughts turned to Portia, and what she might be doing now without him.

Six

"You have a longer reach. You should be able to best him easily, Keith!" Lina called.

"Widald is so much stronger. Hit him harder, Widald, and you will surely win!" Arlie said.

Portia found her sisters watching a mock battle in the practice yard between two young men who were surprisingly evenly matched. She observed them for a few moments before she realised the men were not really battling at all. All that flexing of muscles, fighting without armour or even shirts, and blows that did not seem to land was a show to impress the two girls. A show that was working, judging by Arlie's gasps and Lina's white-knuckled hands as she clutched them to her chest.

"Your turn," Widald whispered. He hooked Keith's wooden practice sword out of his hand and sent it spinning across the yard, scattering chickens that squawked in protest.

"I yield," Keith said thickly. At some point, Widald must have landed a blow to Keith's nose, for it was still bleeding.

"You won!" Arlie dashed across the yard and wrapped her arms around Widald, who grinned at Keith over Arlie's head.

Lina beckoned to Keith. "Let me see to your wounds."

Keith winked back at Widald.

Portia pursed her lips and waited. When her sisters' ministrations culminated in an invitation to dinner that both men eagerly accepted, she knew the wait would soon be over. Sure enough, the men left the yard to put their weapons away.

"Does my father know you are trying to seduce my sisters?" Portia asked.

Keith and Widald exchanged glances, then bowed. "No, Lady Portia." Neither seemed to want to look at her.

"What do you think he will say when I tell him?" Portia said.

Widald lifted his head to meet her eyes. "When I ask for Lady Arlie, I would hope Lord Angus supports my suit."

"And mine for Lady Lina," added Keith.

Portia hesitated. They meant to marry her sisters, not simply seduce them? The girls were of an age for it, much like herself, but it had not occurred to her that they might marry so soon. Unlike the slavish daughters of other places, the women of Isla and the other Southern Isles were proud mistresses of their own destiny. They chose their own husbands, or at least most of them did. Even Portia's father could not force her to marry a man not of her choosing. Though the council might put pressure on him and hence her if they had a man in mind.

Perhaps that was why he had left her here – he wanted to discuss possible husbands for her with the council.

"We know how many suitors there are for your hand, Lady Portia. Lina and Arlie might not have the same claim as you, but they are no less beautiful," Keith continued.

Of course they were. The three girls were identical in appearance, if not disposition. Little wonder that people had called them the Three Little Pigs when they were children, for most people couldn't tell them apart.

Her sisters deserved to be happy with men who loved them. They could do much worse than these two. Portia herself might do worse, what with war coming and all. She would not let her choice place Isla in danger.

"I wish you good fortune," Portia said finally, "but not fertility. Not yet." With a sharp look at them, she marched off.

But in the back of her mind, a tiny seed of doubt took root: for the first time, she dreaded her father's return.

Seven

Lord Lewis was the first guest to arrive at Loch Findlugan. His companion was a messenger from King Harald who had much to say to the council. Lord Angus glanced at Rudolf, then took the messenger for a walk around the lakeshore, so that they might discuss weighty matters in private.

Rudolf burned with curiosity as he watched them go, so he jumped when Lord Lewis's arm landed heavily on his shoulder.

"Let them go, boy. We'll find out what they have to say in council, soon enough. Who are you? I don't remember Angus having a son. You look older than those girls of his."

Rudolf gave Lord Lewis his full attention. "I'm Rudolf, Lord Angus's foster son. From Viken."

Lord Lewis clapped him on the back so hard it would have tipped a lesser man over. "Thought so! My mother came from Viken, and insisted on marrying an Islander, for she declared she wanted a man who wasn't a blonde behemoth. She was a shieldmaiden on one of your dragon ships, but she was fonder of the shield than the ship, and she liked my father more than fighting, so when her brothers departed, she stayed."

"Viken women are as fierce as the women here on the islands," Rudolf agreed. "They have the same strong spirit. I'm sure that's why she stayed."

Lord Lewis winked. "Spirited island girls, hmm? Methinks you have one in particular in mind."

For a moment, Rudolf thought he might blush as brightly as Portia. Except no one could outdo Portia at that. He fought to keep his voice light as he said, "I have no bride yet, Lord Lewis. While I am dependent on the kindness of Lord Angus, so far from my family, I have little to offer a lady."

"Hmm." Lord Lewis made a great show of clearing his throat. It was clear he didn't believe Rudolf.

Best to change the topic. "Did your mother ever teach you Viken war games?" Rudolf asked. "I have a chess set I brought from home. Lord Angus and I sometimes play in the evenings. I'd be happy to give you a lesson in how to play, if you like."

Lord Lewis laughed. "I haven't played that in years! Fetch your set, and we'll see who teaches a lesson to who."

Despite his claim of not having played in a long time, Lord Lewis proved a formidable opponent, and Rudolf lost more games than he won. By the time the other lords arrived to occupy Lord Lewis's attention, Rudolf was more than happy to beat a strategic retreat.

Lord Angus caught him packing his chess set deep in the bottom of his saddle bag. "Don't feel too bad. Lord Lewis has such a passion for the game, I have yet to see him lose. If you wish for a fairer match, where you have a chance to win, perhaps you and I can play after the council meets."

Lord Angus was rarely wrong, but this was one occasion Rudolf was happy to tell him so. "Actually, I won several games. Almost half." Rudolf couldn't keep the smugness out of his tone.

Lord Angus laughed. "Then I had best watch out, lest Lewis try to steal you from my household."

"Nothing he has to offer could entice me to agree to that," Rudolf replied. There was no place for him in any household that didn't hold Portia.

Lord Harris hailed Angus, who clapped Rudolf on the shoulder with a vague, "Good man," before he headed off to join his newly arrived friend.

A fleet of fishing boats ferried the assembled lords across the lake to a tiny, bare island where two men were hastily erecting a sort of canopy to keep the rain off. Most of the lords' men had been left on shore with the servants, who busied themselves preparing food for the assembly. The firepit glowed to life and already a pig was turning on the spit, which would hopefully be ready by the time the council meeting was over.

Rudolf expected to be part of the shore party, but Angus had refused to board a boat until Rudolf was on it, so he sat in the bow, facing the green mound that didn't seem grand enough to be Council Island.

The grass grated under the fishing boat's hull. Automatically, Rudolf leaped out onto the waterlogged turf to help pull the craft further out of the water so that Lord Angus wouldn't get his feet wet. Of course, Angus didn't care, for he squelched down right beside Rudolf. "Good show," Angus whispered as he strode past to the top of the hill.

It took Rudolf a moment to realise what Angus meant. The other boats held off, waiting for Angus before they dared to set foot on the holy isle, which had been the place of council meetings for as long as anyone could remember. It was said that the druids and chieftains of a thousand years ago planned their campaigns against foreign armies on this spot.

And he'd been the first to step onto it, not Angus. Why hadn't Angus warned him? Unless he'd wanted Rudolf to precede him...

His suspicion grew stronger as each of the lords landed on the island and left their boats. Some merely glanced at him, while others openly stared. Lord Lewis grinned as though he was privy to Lord Angus's plans. Rudolf wished he'd thought to ask Angus to share his secret. Of course, he'd have had to know there was a secret...

"My friends, lords of the isles, honoured guest." A nod at Rudolf told him Angus meant him. "Welcome once again to Council Island. By now, you should have all received the message from King Donald of Alba..."

Muttering and grumblings erupted from the circle of men. No one liked King Donald, or his message.

Angus cleared his throat. "I, too, have heard it, and I share your discontent. However, for those who might not remember, he has asked for several things. First, that we recognise his claim to the Southern Isles, and acknowledge him as our king. Second, that we pay tribute to him – not just this year, but for every year of his reign. Third, that we provide him with men to fight the war he faces on his southern border."

The grumblings grew louder.

"In exchange, he offers us the opportunity to help him make Alba great again. He will send men to help us drive out the Viken people who have settled among us, and when they are all gone, the men will help us build walls to keep foreign invaders out." Angus held up his hand for silence. "And, he has offered one of his sons as husband for Lady Portia, who he insists must travel to Alba, where she will stay."

Rudolf jumped to his feet. "Portia will never agree to that!" he shouted.

But Angus never heard. Every lord was just as loud, so the cacophony of sound as the rulers vented their displeasure to the sky with shaken fists and colourful language drowned out individual voices. They were a rumble of thunder, heralding the storm to come.

But Angus was not the Lord of Isla for nothing. He waited patiently, letting the men rage until the volume subsided. Slowly, they sank back onto their benches.

All except for Lord Lewis, whose planted feet turned him into a mighty tree that would not be budged. "If you're going to throw out Vikens, then you may start with me," he roared.

Silence fell.

Most of the men looked shocked. Angus's expression never changed. They'd cooked this plan up between them, Angus and Lewis, Rudolf realised, impressed. This could only be the beginning. He settled down to watch what he knew would prove to be an intriguing show.

"My mother was a Viken."

"Mine, too."

"My grandfather came from Viken."

"My sister married one."

Around and around it went, until every man had declared his relationship to some Viken or other. Vikens had lived among the Southern Islanders for centuries, Rudolf knew, so over the last four hundred years, everyone on the islands had some Viken blood in them. It had been a long time since they'd been foreigners to him.

Angus broke the thoughtful silence. "This council made an agreement with the Viken king, an Erik who has long since gone to his heavenly reward. We would share the islands with his people, and they would defend us against invaders. We would stand together to defend our home." He stared around the circle, taking care to meet every set of eyes for a moment until he had them all. "King Harald sits on Erik's throne now, and we no longer share this soil with the council members who met on that fateful day. But we do stand with one of his descendants." Angus motioned for Rudolf to stand. "Prince Rudolf Vargssen is Harald's nephew. He came to my household as a boy, but he is now more than man enough to fight beside us as a member of my family, which he has. Often."

His interrogatory stare swept around the lords again. "King Harald is not here, but his nephew is. Prince Rudolf, what do you advise the council to do?"

He'd caught Rudolf unprepared, and Angus knew it. Rudolf wet his lips. "I would advise…the lords assembled here to honour your agreements. Oathbreakers are reviled on Viken as much as they are here. Is my uncle such a poor ruler that your oaths are worthless to you, and you will choose to buy another king of whom you know nothing? And not just with money and goods. You would buy him with the lives of your men, the virtue of your virgin daughters…for if he sets his sights on the Lady Portia, none of your daughters will be safe. What do we care for the greatness of our neighbours, who would drive a wedge between our combined peoples, and build walls for which there is no need? We do not need Donald or anything he has to offer, and I would advise you to tell him so."

Several men roared their agreement, but others remained silent. When the roars had died down, one man clambered to his feet, tugging his beard as though checking it was secured to his chin.

"You have something to say, Lord Calum?" Angus asked.

The bearded man nodded. "I do. It is clear the boy is Harald's man, however long he has lived under your roof, and of course his loyalty is to his king. To his family."

"I consider Lord Angus as much family as those I left behind in Viken," Rudolf said.

Angus waved him into silence. "Please continue, Lord Calum."

Calum nodded, then said, "I have no desire to be an oathbreaker, but I made no such oath to King Erik or Harald or whoever the Vikens have sitting on their throne. The council who made that long ago oath did so to ensure a lasting peace that we have known for generations. If a similar oath to King Donald now would bring a similar peace, while keeping to old agreements can only lead to war, should we not take the olive branch that is offered, and forge a new agreement?"

Another man rose.

"Lord Roe?" Angus prompted.

Lord Roe inclined his head in acknowledgement. "Donald isn't offering an olive branch. He's handing us a poisoned chalice. There's no promise of peace in his offer. He starts by wanting to make war on our own people, for Viken blood runs in all of our veins. Then he finishes with a demand for our men to fight his wars, which do not concern us. Donald is offering us war where we currently have peace. Harald does not ask for our daughters or our sons – he demands no hostages he can hold against us. I am with Lord Angus!" He sat down, smiling, as the other lords clapped.

All but Calum, whose expression had twisted into a sneer. "You're only kissing Angus's arse so he'll let your lackwit son marry his daughter!" He turned and lifted his tunic, baring his own hairy arse to emphasise his point.

It took several cries of, "Put it away!" and one "No one wants to kiss your hairy butt cheeks, you old walrus!" before Calum finally sat down.

Lord Harris, a giant of a man who didn't need to stand to be taller than the rest, cleared his throat. "Whether we choose Harald or Donald or declare some other poor fool king, I want one thing to be certain. Lady Portia must remain protected here on the Southern Isles, for as long as she lives."

Several men shouted their support, and a grateful Angus called for a vote. In the resulting hubbub, Lewis shuffled close enough to Rudolf to allow him to mutter, "Watch this well. Any man with an unmarried son will side with Angus. Those with none or too many daughters they wish to marry well will take Calum's side."

The lords divided and Lewis kept up his commentary: "Spinster daughter, daughters, doesn't like Vikens because his wife ran off with one, and Calum."

The other men argued loudly with one another, trying to persuade the others to cross to their side.

Rudolf lowered his voice. "Why does Calum hate Angus so much?"

Lewis glanced from one to the other. "Calum thinks he should be Lord of Isla, not his younger brother. But Catriona chose Angus, then died early in their marriage after giving birth to three girls, and Calum has never forgiven him. If Angus supports something,

Calum will oppose it."

Angus counted the men on each side. "The council votes to support Lord Harris's suggestion. My daughter will be protected here on the isles."

"How do you propose to do that?" Calum drawled. "Everyone knows the story of the Three Little Pigs. Locking that girl up is pointless, for she will only escape as soon as it suits her."

Rudolf had long regretted his flippant comment that had resulted in a nickname Portia and her sisters hated. Especially when the story that went with it was now being used so maliciously against her. By her own flesh and blood.

"Find the girl a husband! Then she'll be his responsibility."

Rudolf couldn't tell who had spoken, but he was soon drowned out by offers of sons, nephews, and, in the case of Lord Dand, the young lord himself. He wanted to shout at them all to be silent. Portia would have screamed it, and then delivered a scathing lecture on where they could stash their manhoods, if in fact they still had them when she was done.

Angus had been wise to leave her at home. Rudolf wished he didn't have to witness this.

Lord Lewis cupped his hands to his mouth. "Why not forge an alliance with Harald's family? The young prince here isn't married, so why not make him truly a member of Lord Angus's family by giving him to the girl?"

Rudolf had a sudden vision of himself wrapped in a giant red ribbon, being presented to Portia. At the very least, it would make her laugh.

Angus hushed them. "You have all offered many eligible bachelors for my daughter to consider. But the council has voted to protect her here in the isles, where a woman may choose her own husband. We should each choose our champion, to form a personal bodyguard for her, until that happens. In protecting Lady Portia, they will each have their chance to woo her, if that is their wish."

Now Rudolf wanted to laugh. Hard. Portia would not take the news well when she discovered she was to always be surrounded by a personal honour guard. He sobered when he realised he would be the one who'd have to tell her.

If there was a fate, she was the one laughing at him right now.

Eight

The council meeting dragged on in a series of debates, which ranged from stories the lords had heard about Donald to the difficulties of tithing their own people. This continued until the sun sank low on the horizon, and Rudolf could smell roasting meat from the fire pit on the shore. The fishing boats returned to ferry them across the loch, and Rudolf found himself in the same boat as Lord Ronin, one of the men who had stood beside Calum in the vote about Portia. At first, Rudolf wondered at the man's motive, but Ronin soon enlightened him. Just as Lewis had said, he was a man with many unmarried daughters, and an opportunity to sell them to an eligible bachelor like Rudolf was something Lord Ronin did not intend to miss.

Thankfully the boat trip was short, and Rudolf managed to avoid Ronin for the rest of the evening.

After talking all day, the lords still had plenty to say, though they spoke of more mundane matters. Daughters and wives, sons and servants, sheep and seals, cattle and crops. Rudolf had little to add to any of these subjects, so he simply listened.

Eventually, they all retired early, for they knew it would be another gruelling day on the morrow.

The second day started with less of a show than the first, for Rudolf knew to hang back and let Angus go first. The debate resumed, and Rudolf wished he hadn't come. Day after day, they droned on, seeming to get no closer to a plan of action than they were on the day they began. Yet there were useful suggestions amid the filibustering. Slowly but surely, each man realised what Portia had known instantly: that whatever action they took, it would lead to war.

Sometime on the fifth day, Rudolf was roused from his doze by an elbow administered to his ribs. He instantly regretted his late-night chess match with Lewis, whose sharp elbow was probably a dig at revenge for Rudolf's win last night. Feeling the entire council's eyes on him, Rudolf ventured, "Could you repeat that?"

Angus looked amused. "The council would like to know what kind of assistance King Harald will offer us in this matter. Can you tell us what kind of army he has at his disposal?"

Rudolf spread his arms wide and shrugged. "I have no idea. I was a boy when I left Viken, and I know more of your strengths than I do of my uncle's. Men have died in battle, old men who did not have retired. Boys have become men, and taken the places that belong to greybeards. To know my uncle's true strength, you would have to ask him."

Lord Harris said, "Never mind the numbers, then. Do you believe your uncle will offer men to help defend the isles against Donald?"

Angus stared at him hungrily, expectantly. Rudolf wished he knew what the man wanted him to say.

But he did not, so what Rudolf said was, "I would have to ask him."

Angus jumped in before any of the other lords could. "But a request from his nephew, his own blood, for warriors and weapons would be received far more favourably than anything from the rest of us. I propose that Rudolf make contact with his kinsman in order to enlist his support." Angus surveyed the circle. "Any man who doesn't agree, raise a hand."

Only Calum's hand waved like that of a drowning man for a moment before dropping limply into his lap, defeated. Angus produced a scroll and began to read from it. Amid all the waffling, Angus had paid attention to every word of their discussion. And from it, he had distilled a powerful liquor that would become their brave plan for the future.

Defences would be shored up, more weapons would be made, supplies of food and drink would be stored, and they would remain vigilant. There was no mention of Donald or even Harald.

In short, they would do nothing new. They would continue as they always had, preparing for an attack that might never come, but remaining in readiness for when it did.

The collected lords gave their assent to the plan, though Calum was predictably silent.

It was with considerable relief that Rudolf left the island for good, hoping never to return.

That night they feasted, celebrating their decision as much as the opportunity to see their friends again. For life held many uncertainties, especially with the threat of war, and who knew when they might share bread and meat again?

The ale flowed freely until Calum burst into a surprisingly familiar song. Even Rudolf joined in, though he did not know all the words. The song ended but the singing continued late into the night as all good feasts should. Rudolf grew brave enough to offer some songs from his homeland, though he found he had forgotten many of the words. By night's end, they all sang the same song, for at the bottom of a barrel of ale, all words sound the same anyway.

The next morning, Angus found Rudolf dunking his pounding head in the loch in the hope that the icy waters might wash away some of the cursed ale that still swam behind his eyes.

Rudolf rose and flicked the wet hair off his face. "Good morning, Lord Angus," he said. He glanced behind Angus to find a man he did not know. "And this is…?"

"Gustav Gustavssen, a messenger sent by the King of Viken. He came to summon you home." Angus looked as though the words pained him.

Rudolf did not believe it. "But I promised Portia…"

Angus sighed. "Portia will wait. More important is the help we seek from your uncle. I always knew this day would come, though Varg said it would not. Your King has need of you, and so do we. A message he might ignore, but you? He cannot. Tell him what we face.

Tell him that we are loyal. Tell him everything that took place during your time here. Tell him we were honoured to host you, and that we would be happy to host you again for as long as you wish to stay. You and any Viken men you bring with you." Only now did the worry show in Angus's eyes. "Please, Rudolf. If you have any loyalty or affection for me or my family, I beg you to do this for us."

The lump in Rudolf's throat made it hard to speak. Yet speak he must. "I will," he vowed. He squeezed his eyes shut, forcing out the words that cost him so much to say. "Protect Portia for me. That is all I ask. Protect Portia for me and I promise I will return with all the men I can muster."

Angus bowed his head. "I swear I will."

Rudolf said his farewells with the rest, smiling and nodding to hide the heavy heart within. By the time the sun was high in the sky, Rudolf was resigned. He would follow Gustav the stranger to his fate.

Nine

Portia met her father in the yard, barefoot and out of breath from running. "What happened? Will we be safe?" She peered around her father and her face fell. "Where is Dolf?"

"The council has decided to refuse Donald's demands. They have also sent a message to Harald, the Viken king, asking for reinforcements should Donald choose to invade." Angus sighed, a sound that sank beneath the weighty worries of all the world, or at least the Southern Isles. "Rudolf insisted on carrying the message to the king himself."

Portia didn't want to believe it. "He's gone to Viken? Why? And without saying goodbye?"

"Sailing takes time, and Donald could arrive at any moment. Or he might not arrive at all. Better to have King Harald's help sooner rather than later. Rudolf asked me to tell you goodbye, and to ask you to take care of his things until his return."

Her father might not know it, but his eyes wouldn't meet hers when he lied, just like now.

Portia took a deep, shuddering breath, forcing back the sobs that threatened to choke her.

Rudolf would not come back, and there would be war.

"What must we do to prepare Isla for the coming war?" Portia asked.

Father brightened. "During the council meeting, I made a list. Let's go through it together, shall we?"

He extracted a scroll from his saddlebag and Portia steeled herself for the storm to come.

Ten

The bustling harbour of Portnahaven seemed like another world after the strange solemnity that shrouded Council Island and Loch Findlugan. Rudolf almost wanted to turn back, to see if he could capture the spirit of the place to carry with him across the ocean. For the first time in many years, he felt afraid of what was to come.

He had so much he wanted to do with his life, and none of it involved a return to Viken right now. He burned to know why Harald had summoned him. He'd lived on Isla for so long, he thought they might have forgotten about him.

Yet Gustav was proof that they had not.

People stared at Rudolf and Gustav, as though they had never seen a Viken before. Which couldn't be the case, for two Viken longboats lay in the harbour.

A skinny boy called out from the mast of a merchant vessel, "Are you going to fight the dragon for the princess?"

Rudolf laughed at the thought that even cabin boys believed in fairytales. "No, there are no dragons left in the world, boy. Heroes have slayed them all."

"Not this one! He devours sheep and maidens and the king has offered half his kingdom and a whole princess to the man who brings him the dragon's head!"

A likely tale, though one that was widespread, for even the men on the longboats had heard of it. The details differed widely, but three things remained – the dragon, the half kingdom, and the whole princess.

Word had reached Viken, too, before their arrival. All people could talk about was this dragon. No one seemed to know or care about a looming war for the Southern Isles.

Rudolf paid far too high a price for a horse to carry him to the castle gates, where he drew to a halt, not willing to enter in case it was still Regina's realm. He was not afraid of many women, but Harald's queen had wanted to kill him as a child.

He addressed one of the guards: "Is the king at home? I carry an urgent message from the Southern Isles."

The guard shook his head. "No, he's up in the borderlands, dealing with some Opplanders. He rides at the head of his army – he shouldn't be hard to find."

Harald leading the army? "What about Varg?" Rudolf asked eagerly. Wherever the army was, he would find its commander – his father.

"Varg fell in battle not long ago. That's why the king commands the army now."

Dead? Rudolf received the news like a punch to the gut. He wanted to double over and howl in pain, but he knew he could not. So he straightened, stiffened, and said, "Thank you."

He turned his horse away from the gate, and headed for the road to Oppland, and the borderlands in between. It wasn't until he was alone in the empty road that he felt the first tear fall.

He was all that was left of his family, and he would never see his father again. Never know if his father was proud of the man he'd become.

More than anything, he wished himself back on Isla, with Angus and Portia. Angus would know what to say to make him feel whole again, and Portia would be sure to hug him until the hole this loss left in his heart had healed over.

He would have settled for just Portia, feeling her soft body against his as their embrace became more intimate, her soft sigh as she yielded to him as she'd yielded to no one else and…

Rudolf cursed. Now he had a raging hard-on, a hole where his heart used to be, a horse which didn't want to do anything he told it to, and a king to find. Who might kill him on sight, to please his queen.

Oh, fate would be rolling around on the floor, she must be laughing to hard at him now.

Grimly, Rudolf rode on.

Eleven

"I caught them showing off for the girls in the practice yard, so I warned them, but Keith and Widald would not listen. I caught Keith kissing Lina in the stillroom several times and I lost count of the number of times Arlie came to dinner with bits of grass or hay stuck to her underdress. Both men said they had honourable intentions and talked of marriage, but I'm afraid – "

Father cut Portia off. "Afraid your sisters might be doing things only married women do? Well, you're all of an age for it. I shouldn't be so surprised. I like having you girls at home so much I admit I've waited longer than I should have to find husbands for you all, but perhaps I have waited long enough. Both Keith and Widald are worthy sons of loyal men. I take it your sisters are fond of them?"

Portia's mouth hung open. Her father wanted to reward them for seducing her sisters? "Y-yes," she stammered. "At least, I think so. Lina seemed happy about the kissing, but Arlie only blushed when I asked about the hay."

"Good, good," Father said. "I'll speak to the men myself. If your sisters agree, I will need your help planning the wedding. As soon as possible, I would imagine."

"Yes, Father." Portia struggled to moisten her dry mouth. "What about me? If I were to…find some man I liked kissing, would you be as happy for me to marry him as you are for Lina and Arlie?" She already knew the answer, but she prayed he might be more forthcoming about who he did want her to marry instead.

Angus sighed. "Portia. You know it is different for you. I would hope that you would stop at just kissing, and not let your feelings get in the way of what is best for you, and Isla. There is a lot riding on the man you choose to marry, and with war coming…we must wait and see. A marriage alliance to the right man at the right time might save us. You are too precious to waste. Instead, I must keep you safe. I have spoken to the other lords on the council, and they have agreed to send some of their best warriors to be your personal guard. They will arrive…"

Father kept talking, but Portia stopped listening.

Inwardly, she breathed a sigh of relief that she would not be asked to marry any man yet.

When the time came, she would do what was best for Isla and the rest of the Southern Isles, but was it too much to ask that she might be allowed to marry for love?

Twelve

Shouts and singing rang out across the valley, punctuated by calls for more ale. Rudolf was surely home, for that was the sound he remembered most. He'd had to sneak into the feasts he'd remembered, for he'd been too young to attend as a full man before he'd left Viken for the Southern Isles, but now he was a man he could take part in full measure.

Would they remember him? Accept him as the man he'd become, or think of him as the boy who'd been banished to the ends of the earth to keep him away from the throne that blood bound him to the same way it bound Reidar, his cousin, the man Regina insisted would be the king's heir?

They toasted the king's health and courage and long life, fearless roars echoing into the night. This was a victory feast, then, for they didn't fear an enemy hearing them.

A cheer rose up, then the bonfire flared as someone threw more fuel on top. Now he could see them – a band of men, mostly sitting, though some stood by, and a servant crouched beside a barrel to fill a cup of ale.

He'd not tasted Viken ale since he was a boy, and even those sips had been stolen, burning down his throat as he fought not to gag at the taste. Reidar had claimed to like it, but then he'd been older, bolder, closer to manhood.

Someone peered into the darkness, as though he knew someone watched them.

It was now or never.

He dug his knees into his horse's side, not wanting to be caught creeping. He was a Viken warrior as much as any of these men, growing up with the same songs they roared even now.

So why did this not feel like home?

He burst into their circle. "I must see the king!" he said, surveying the surprised faces, ale cups hanging halfway to gaping mouths.

He slid from his skittish horse. The foolish beast kicked up sparks with its hooves, frightening itself further. Not for the first time, Rudolf missed the palfrey Lord Angus had given him on Isla. Hector would have known how to make a proper entrance, though now he was in Portia's care, the horse would have no need to do so.

So Rudolf planted his feet as firmly as he'd tried to teach Portia, a memory that lent strength to his tone when he demanded, "Where is the king? 'Twas he who summoned me."

But King Harald was not here. These men were all strangers. Rudolf had been away too long. No sign of recognition on anyone's expression, as hands dropped to the dagger-hilts and axe handles. Then his eyes met the piercing gaze of the man by the ale barrel.

A man who stood straight and tall, no longer crouched like a servant fetching a drink.

"Reidar!" Rudolf cried in relief.

The boy had broadened, even aged a little, but there was no mistaking his cousin, or the way he lifted the cup of ale to his own lips. Reidar served no one; the heir to the throne had no need to kneel.

For a moment, Reidar could have been the Lord of Isla, pausing to take stock before delivering some weighty judgement. This was not the boy who'd hunted boar with careless courage so many years ago. This was a man who meant to be king.

And for the first time, Rudolf didn't care. Reidar could have his throne. Together with his horse, Rudolf had left his heart in Portia's safekeeping, on Isla. Though the girl did not know it yet.

"Cousin!" Rudolf cried, folding a resisting Reidar into his manly embrace. "It is good to see you. Where is the king?"

Loud laughter greeted him from all sides, and Rudolf realised his mistake. If Harald was not here and all those he'd spoken to swore the king rode at the head of this army, then the crown had passed to Reidar.

Uncertainty crossed Reidar's face for the first time – ah, there was a boy beneath the king still, though he tried to hide it. "Rudolf?" His grin of recognition was everything Rudolf could have hoped for. "I thought you'd sailed off the western edge of the world!"

The men around him relaxed, whispering to each other that he was Prince Varg's son, the other royal prince. Now the hostile eyes turned expectant.

Rudolf racked his brain for what they might expect of him. Gifts? Plunder? He had neither, for he hadn't gone raiding. It took him a moment to recollect that the people of Viken were no different to those of Isla when a traveller came to visit – they wanted to hear new tales.

So he kept his voice deliberately light as he spun a tale of paradise found at the Southern Isles. And the beauty of its women, though he didn't dare mention Portia by name.

Reidar's expression darkened at the mention of women.

Rudolf quickly changed topic to talk about the gossip in every port – the Kasmirus dragon that no man could slay.

Even that did not cheer Reidar.

Realising he was rapidly wearing out what little welcome Reidar offered, Rudolf bowed his head in memory of Harald. "I am sorry for your loss, cousin. Your father was a good king, and a wise one, too." After all, it had been King Harald's command that had sent him to the Southern Isles, even if he knew it had been his father's idea. Both men had seen how close the cousins were – like brothers, as far apart in age as Harald and Varg themselves. Yet Rudolf had faithfully promised his father that he would return to serve Reidar when his cousin became king.

Realisation dawned more suddenly than any sunrise. If Harald had died so recently, then he had been the one to summon Rudolf home, knowing Reidar would need him. Perhaps Harald had not had a chance to tell Reidar. With Regina pouring poison into Reidar's ear about Rudolf's desire for the throne, Reidar probably suspected Rudolf was here to make a claim for the kingship.

If Rudolf couldn't convince him of his

loyalty to the crowned king, Reidar could have him killed before he could return to Portia and fulfil his promise to her. Rudolf knew himself to be a capable fighter, but he was no match for an army. He was here to fight alongside his countrymen, not against them. Did Reidar know that? Or was he little more than Regina's puppet…and Rudolf would be forced to claim the crown he did not want?

"Why else would he send me to the ends of the earth to learn warcraft from some foreign lord?" Rudolf forced out a laugh to hide his pain at speaking so ill of Lord Angus. But needs must, if he was to win Reidar's trust. "I can tell you tales of tactics their men use in battle that we would never think of. I would not have believed them, had I not seen it with my own eyes."

"Battle tactics? But Mother said – "

"Is Aunt Regina still around? She will outlive us all, that battle axe will. I remember she caught me sitting on your father's throne once. She clouted me over the ear and gave me such a tongue lashing I couldn't open my mouth in her presence for a year. She said if she ever caught me sitting there again, she'd thrash my backside until I had nothing left to sit on!" Rudolf laughed as though it was all a joke to him, though it had not been to Regina. No, the queen would never forgive the slight to her son.

So Regina still lived. Pity. Her son would stand stronger without her. Even Rudolf knew that. But if he could pry Reidar away from her, perhaps he might still be a good king. He and Reidar had been like brothers, and the boy he'd known was no lapdog. The man before him might still be a stranger.

A stranger who doubted him.

Rudolf met Reidar's gaze steadily. Perhaps sending him away had made Rudolf the stronger man after all. The true king could not walk away from this meeting as the loser, though he did not need to win.

Almost as though Reidar could read his mind, the king gave a slight nod. It was decided – whatever it was.

Reidar cleared his throat, raising his voice so the assembled men might hear. "Tomorrow, we ride west, to where there are reports of a foreign force waiting to ambush us. In three days' time, we shall go into battle. Will you join us, cousin?"

A challenge, and a fight. Reidar knew what he was about. Even if he'd wanted to, Rudolf couldn't refuse. "The Southern Isles may have softened me, but beneath it beats a Viken heart still!" Rudolf declared. "I will fight at your side like we did as boys."

"Ale for my cousin! We must toast his return!" Reidar roared.

Another man filled the cup – not Reidar this time – but it was Reidar the man handed it to, and Reidar who then presented it to Rudolf. A masterful piece of theatre.

But Rudolf was better versed in such things. Regina would never have allowed her precious son to play-act, but Portia and her sisters had pulled him into their playing as often as they could.

Rudolf took the offered cup with both hands as though it held the blood of the saviour himself. He held it aloft as he knelt before Reidar, praying he wouldn't spill any. It wouldn't do to splash the king's shoes. He raised his voice to a shout that matched Reidar's for volume. "Nay, a toast to my cousin, the new King of Viken. May his reign be long and filled with so many victories the bards forget to sing of anyone else!"

Silence reigned for a long moment as the other men waited to see their king's reaction. Rudolf barely caught the tiny nod, but it was there. Reidar might not be perfectly comfortable in the role yet, but he was definitely their king.

The men shouted, raising their own cups to second Rudolf's toast.

Only then did they offer him a place at the fire. And Rudolf took it, pleased to be accepted back into the land of his ancestors.

A land that was no longer home.

Thirteen

If there was one good thing about the threat of war, it was that Portia's archery skills improved. The finger guards Rudolf had given her clung like a second skin even as they protected her, while she loosed arrow after arrow at a target so full of holes it resembled cork instead of wood.

"Portia."

Portia lowered her bow. "Yes, Father?"

"I have some men you must meet."

Sighing, she unstrung her bow, knowing she would have no more time for practice if they had guests.

Sure enough, the hall seemed full of men — young, loud and dressed in their best armour. Lords' sons, she guessed. Now, more than ever, she ached with loss at Rudolf's leaving. He would have greeted the men and deflected their acquisitive stares. Without him, she had the distinct impression they regarded her like a succulent leg of lamb. That desire to devour.

Portia shivered, then straightened. She was the lady of this hall, and her welcome must honour the ancient laws of hospitality that bound them all. "Good day, and welcome to my father's hall," she said.

The men stumbled all over each other to bow.

"We thank you, Lady Portia," said a man with hair as red as her own. "I certainly think I will enjoy my stay here." He made no effort to hide his approval as he looked her up and down.

Like he was buying a lamb for slaughter, Portia thought uneasily.

Angus edged into the hall beside her. "The council agreed that you deserved a guard of your own to protect you, now Rudolf has returned to Viken. Each of the lords offered one of their best fighting men to be your protector. With the prospect of war, I thought it prudent to accept their offers. All of them."

Best fighting men? Portia gave a breathy snort as she surveyed the newly puffed-out chests and proudly lifted heads. Finest fighters indeed. These were men who did not realise guard duty was nothing to be proud of. Men their lords would not miss. They were certainly no true replacement for Rudolf.

"Welcome to my father's household, then," she said, fighting to hide her fury. She turned to her father. "May I return to the practice field, please?"

With her father's permission, she marched back outside and across the field to the target. She ripped the arrows out, not caring if they took chunks of wood with them. She'd ask for a new target when she'd shot this one to pieces – next week, at this rate.

Her arms filled with arrows, she turned and found the band of men watching her from the edge of the field. Had they never seen a girl shoot before?

She let the arrows clatter to the sod at her feet, then strung her bow. If they wanted to watch, so be it. She would give them a show.

Notch, draw, aim, breathe, loose. It was Rudolf's voice whispering the words in her head.

Loose.

Loose.

Loose.

Unbidden, a smile warmed her lips. It was almost like having him here beside her once more.

"Lady Portia?"

This whisper was not Rudolf.

"Lady Portia, I just wanted to say that you have no need to defend yourself now, for I would be delighted to do it for you. My sword is always ready."

Portia followed his gaze to his sword hilt, raising her eyebrows at the tent his other sword had pitched beneath his tunic. "So I see," she said drily, turning away. Her next arrow skimmed across the top of the target.

As she notched another arrow, an arm

snaked around her waist. "Lady Portia, if you will permit me to assist you. I am a skilled archer, and I always hit my mark." His hand drifted higher, headed for her breast.

Portia stomped on the man's foot and twisted out of his embrace. "Not today, thank you." Not ever.

Her next arrow fell short of the target.

A heavy hand landed on her shoulder. "Lady Portia, if you but lift the bow a little higher – "

Portia whirled, drawing the bow back. The heavy handed one backed up so quickly he almost landed on his arse. She pointed her arrow at each man in turn, punctuating her words. "The next man who says my name or touches me is going to get an arrow through his manhood. And no matter how small that target might be, I will not miss."

When no one moved, she added, "Didn't your fathers warn you about me?"

Now they backed up a few steps. All but one man, who held his ground.

Portia aimed her arrow at the stubborn one.

He bowed deeply. "My father, Lord Lewis,

did indeed warn me about you. He said that one day soon, we would all be forced to fight for our homes, as foreign kings battle over who owns us. And not just us. King Donald offered his son to be your husband, and King Harald will undoubtedly do the same. As the Lady of Isla, you are at the very heart of our people, of our home. When you marry, the council will crown your husband not as Lord of Isla, but as our king. None of us deserves that honour. Not yet. We are here to defend your honour, because to lose you is to lose all the Southern Isles." Now he straightened and lifted his chin, so that he might meet her eyes. "Lady Portia, I will defend you with my life. And any man here who thinks he has the right to seduce you against your will, a lady who is courted by kings, will have to get through me." He marched across the no man's land and planted his feet firmly in the middle ground between Portia and her would-be suitors. He drew his sword, then threw it on the ground, followed by his dagger. "Go on. If you think you're man enough to be king, fight me!"

His first opponent was the biggest of them,

as broad and tall as Rudolf. He bunched one meaty fist and swung it at young Lewisson.

Lewisson dodged. His elbow swung behind him slightly before he jabbed his own fist into the giant's midsection. The man went down, with Lewisson on top of him.

They rolled on the ground, kicking and punching, until someone said thickly, "Yield!"

The two men broke apart. Only then could see Lewisson was the victor while the other man limped away, pressing a hand to his bleeding nose.

Lewisson's second opponent charged at him while his back was turned. Portia shouted a warning, but the stocky man bulled into Lewisson just as he turned to face him, too late to keep his balance. Lewisson grabbed him as he fell, so they both tumbled to the ground together. They wrestled for some time, each trying to break the other man's ribs as they rocked first one way, then the other.

"Enough!" Angus roared.

Lewisson rolled away from his opponent. He still had the presence of mind to place himself between the other men and Portia.

"You're here to protect the lady, not fight amongst yourselves. I have your oaths, boys. Break them, and I will send you home in disgrace."

Most of the men ducked the heads, shamefaced. Boys indeed.

All except Lewisson.

Portia held out her hand to help him up.

He laughed, waving away her offer of assistance as he clambered to his feet. He wiped away a trickle of blood from his split lip. "My father forgot to warn me about how beautiful you are, Lady Portia. Now I see why a war will be fought for you."

Portia shook her head. Her voice was chilly as she said, "Not for me. For my home."

He inclined his head. "As you say. We all fight for something. I will fight for your honour and mine, Lady, but I have more at stake than most. I am the youngest son of Lord Lewis, to be sure, but I was fostered at Rum Isle with Lord Ronin and his daughters. Lady Rhona and I have...an understanding, I suppose you would call it. Her father had no men to send to serve you, so he sent me. If I serve you well, Rhona and I will be allowed to marry when I go home."

Portia's expression softened into a smile. "I'm sure you will. I pray that Lady Rhona will have you home soon."

His answering smile was bleak. "If my father is right, as he usually is, this war will be long and bitter. You will have need of every man among us to defend you. But at the end, I hope to invite you and your husband to my wedding."

"Thank you." Portia remembered her manners. "What is your name?"

His eyes widened, and he bowed low. "Forgive my rudeness. Lady Portia, I am Grieve Lewisson, foster son to Lord Ronin." He straightened. "I should probably let you get back to your archery practice. You set an example we should all follow." Grieve turned and cupped his hands to his mouth. "Oi, you lot. You can't expect Lady Portia to shoot all the invaders herself. Get your bows and show the lady you can do more than stand around looking pretty and staring at her arse!" He reddened. "Sorry, my lady. Your bottom, I meant."

Portia waved away both the swearing and the apology. Instead, she watched in wonder as the other men hurried to obey Grieve.

They soon had a row of targets, bristling with arrows.

Grieve roared, "Cease fire!" He waited for the bows to lower before he pointed at the targets. "Right, retrieve!"

Portia marched across the field with the rest of them to refill her quiver. Out the corner of her eye, she watched Grieve as he walked the line of targets, offering advice to the others. Most of the men nodded in response.

So that was how you commanded men, she thought. Idly, she wondered if Rudolf would be as capable. He was no lord or lord's son, but there was something about him that made you want to follow him.

Grieve appeared at her side. "Do you need help with those, my lady?"

Too late, Portia realised she'd been so busy watching him, she'd forgotten about her arrows. Her face grew hot.

"No, but thank you," she said.

She might not have Rudolf, but Grieve might be a suitable substitute. At least for a while.

Fourteen

Rudolf had never liked the wait before a battle began. His armour hugged him like a protective parent, though he wished he'd forgone his helm for this battle. He wanted to see things clearly, and he was willing to risk his head to do so. Truth be told, he wanted to see how his cousin fought, and generalled the battle, but Reidar had placed him on one wing while the king himself stood in the other. Once the fighting began, he wouldn't be able to see across the Opplander army, for their men stood as tall as Vikens. Well, they must be kin, however distant, if they thought to claim Reidar's throne.

That, or fools who didn't care if they died.

Rudolf surveyed the Viken army. The Opplanders were fools indeed, no matter whose kin they were.

A roar rose up, commanding the Vikens to charge. As though they were one man, they did, Reidar with them.

Rudolf swore and took off at a run.

The king leading the charge? To hell with the Opplanders. Surely Reidar could not be such a fool as to believe he was like the great hero kings of old?

Rudolf blocked an attack that came in from the side, taking it on his shield as his sword slid below to gut the man before he could strike again. Rudolf pulled his sword free and kept running.

An axe came at him and he twisted away, but not before it took a chunk out of his shield. The man tried to raise his axe again for a better blow, but Rudolf was faster. The men of the Southern Isles sometimes fought barehanded, and when they did, they fought dirty. His boot caught the man in his midsection, folding him in half. He screamed as his axe bit into his own flesh, but Rudolf leaped over him and ran on.

Another axe clattered across his shield, badly thrown, followed by the arm of the unfortunate axeman. His corpse must be one of those littering the ground, a carpet of groaning, crawling dead, the like of which Rudolf had been told dwelled in hell. Something squashed and spurted beneath his foot, but Rudolf didn't care. His only care was his cousin, the king.

A giant of a man came at him, two hands clenched around his axe haft as he swung it in a deadly arc.

The blade took off the head of the Viken beside Rudolf, slowing for but a moment before coming to collect his.

Rudolf was faster. He ran at the giant and slashed upward with his dagger, aiming for the man's unprotected throat. Blood bubbled, but not before the axe finished its half-circle swing, for the weapon had a momentum of its own. Down went the giant, with Rudolf on top of him, pinned to the dying man by the axe handle across his back.

Rudolf stabbed again, determined to fight his way free. The giant screamed, gurgled, then stilled. Rudolf wiped the gelatinous globe that had once been the giant's eye off his blade before he rose.

He had a moment to see someone slice Reidar's side before another axe-wielding giant blocked his way. Rudolf hated giants.

"Protect the king!" Rudolf bellowed to the men around him as he lifted his sword to meet the down-swinging axe. Something squelched under his foot and a surprised Rudolf slid several feet before he stopped, now behind the giant who'd wanted to cleave him in two.

Now, there was nothing between him and Reidar, except the king's opponent, whose axe blade was red with Reidar's blood.

Rudolf broke into a run, lifting his sword to run the man through. Perhaps he should have slowed, for his blade went straight through the man's throat as he turned to avoid a sword wielded by another of the king's men. It mattered not. The king was alive, and his opponent was dead.

Reidar eyes were wide with a panic Rudolf shared. Yes, he had almost died. "Thank you," Reidar said.

Rudolf longed to tell him to leave the battlefield to his more than capable men, but Reidar would not welcome a command from his cousin, however well meant. So all he said was, "Any time, my king," before he turned away to take on another Opplander.

Out of the corner of his eye, Rudolf saw Reidar leave the field of his own volition, not as a coward, but as a general walking among his troops. The battle was almost won, anyway – only a few Opplanders remained.

Including one last giant, who charged up to Rudolf as though he was a human battering ram. "You killed my brothers!" he shouted.

Rudolf didn't see the man's axe strapped to his back until it came up in a deadly arc he was too slow to dodge, though he knew it would cleave through his head, helm and all. So he grabbed the giant's arm instead, and hung on with all his weight.

Then the axe blow landed, and the world

went black.

Fifteen

Father threw the scroll down on the table with a sigh. "Portia, do we have everything we need to put on a lavish feast? The sort we'd do for an important guest?"

Portia's heart leaped within her. "A guest?"

With her sisters married and gone to live with their husbands, that left just her and Father in the huge longhouse, and sometimes not even him, when another council meeting was called. Oh, she had her men, as Father called them, but they slept in the barracks across the yard. A barracks they'd built, to protect her honour, they said, though she suspected she had Grieve to thank for that.

He had this habit of asking her, oh so politely, every morning how she'd slept. After one particularly noisy night, she'd confessed that the men's snoring had kept her awake, and they'd started building the barracks that very afternoon.

They had settled down to do what they'd been sent here for - protecting her. Protecting her from what, Portia wasn't sure. Herself, maybe. Not that they had much to protect her from. The most dangerous thing to occur in all their time guarding her had happened yesterday, when her bowstring had snapped and sliced her arm. Rudolf would have seen the thinning string and told her to replace it long ago, she was sure of it, but he was still in Viken, and she was here with...her men.

Unless he was the guest.

Father sighed. He did far too much of that lately, and his smiles were more rare than summer snow. "Donald keeps sending more messages, and the council refuses to respond. In the last one, he said he would send envoys that we could not ignore. According to this missive, his envoy has arrived at Isla, and he invokes the ancient laws of hospitality for us to welcome the man."

Laws the Islanders obeyed, but would the foreigners? Portia wondered. Sharing bread and meat with someone under your roof gave them guest right, the right to your protection for as long as they stayed. Accepting this hospitality then gave the guest an obligation to honour the host. Neither could take up arms against one another while they dwelled under the same roof. Twenty years had passed, but people still spoke about the day Calum had struck her father at a feast. Portia had only been a baby at the time, and her father still grieving her mother's death, but she knew the details as though she'd been there.

Calum had arrived late, when everyone else was seated. He'd marched into her father's hall, and levelled him with one blow before accusing him of murdering Portia's mother. He'd remained in the hall only long enough to seize the remains of a ham which he swung by his side as he marched out, never to return.

When Nurse had told it, she'd added some fanciful embellishments of her own. Calum's eyes had glistened with tears, and his usually cleanshaven face had been shadowed with stubble. He'd never shaved since, Nurse said. Or that he'd called down a curse on Angus as he departed, swearing he would lose everyone he loved, a fitting fate for Catriona's killer. Then he'd choked on the ham and she'd had to save him.

Given how many times she'd had to save Arlie from choking on whatever food she tried to swallow whole in her eagerness to eat, Portia had believed it.

"Portia?"

Portia shook her head. "Mm?"

"I said he will be here by nightfall. Do we have sufficient supplies for a feast, or will we need to send for more?" Angus asked with a bite of impatience in his tone.

It was Portia's turn to sigh. Lina would know, if she were here. She would have enough on hand to feed every man on Isla. "I will ask the cook." She turned to go.

Father caught her arm, his grip gentle but

firm. "Keep your men near all the time now. I fear you will have need of them."

Her father was rarely wrong, and there was no point in arguing. "Yes, Father." At least she wouldn't be lonely.

She buried herself in preparations for the impromptu celebration that she had no heart for, so deeply that when she heard the clop of hooves on the road, she was surprised to find the sky fading into dusk.

It sat ill with her to set a place for Donald's man at her father's right hand, for that was Rudolf's place, though it had been years since he'd last sat there.

Would he ever return?

"My lady, are you well?" Grieve's voice cut through her grief.

Portia nodded and wiped her eyes. "Of course. A mote of dust in my eye, is all. Blown up from the road, as our guests approach. We should take our places in the hall before the dust in the yard gets worse with so many men and horses." She lifted her chin turned her gaze on the open doors to the hall.

Donald's envoy shuffled inside like a seal

walking on its tail flukes. A wide, grey column of a man, tapering only at his feet. A gold medallion suspended from a thick, gold chain was his only badge of office, distinguishing him from the other members of his small party.

When the envoy reached the dais that held the lord's table, Father rose, spreading his arms to offer a traditional welcome.

"You call this a hall?" the seal man complained. "I wouldn't keep pigs in this." He sniffed. "And where is the girl?"

Father hesitated for only a moment, but it was long enough for Portia to feel his anger build. Not that he let it show in his voice. "Sir, I welcome you to our humble home, where you will be offered every hospitality. I am Lord Angus of Isla, and this is the Lady Portia, of whose famed beauty I'm sure you have heard much."

And woe betide him if he hadn't, Portia added silently.

"That plain, freckled lass looks nothing like a lady, or a beauty. Prince Malcolm will be most disappointed. He'll have to bed her in the dark with his eyes closed. If she's the best you have, your women must all be uglier than this hall. I'm surprised King Donald thinks you are worthy allies at all. Savages like you people don't deserve to own land."

Portia rose, her blood heated to boiling within her. "And I am surprised you are fool enough to insult a man in his own hall, when his men outnumber you so. King Donald must be even more of a fool to send you as an envoy, unless he dislikes you so much he wants you to die."

The envoy paled, tugging at his collar as he licked his lips. "Tame your sow, Angus, and teach her to be silent, or Prince Malcolm will cut out her tongue."

"My lady," Grieve whispered. "Might I recommend – "

"No, you may not," Portia hissed. Only two men could tell her what to do. Rudolf, who was not here, and –

"Portia, please," Angus said.

Portia sat down, glaring at the envoy.

Angus continued, "Will you accept our offer of hospitality…ah, I do not believe I caught your name, sir."

"You may call me Lord Mason, for if a hall such as this makes you a lord, then I am surely one twice over, for I have a castle and my cousin is a captain in the king's guard," the pale-faced seal said with shaky grandeur.

A nobody, then, and Portia had guessed right. Donald did not care if this man lived or died.

Yet her father sat the nobody beside him in the place of honour and served him first.

Mason's complaints continued:

"This lamb is too tough."

"We only give such food to pigs."

"Why have you no music in this hall?"

Portia choked at the third one. Men sang when they were merry, and deep in their cups. Not when they waited for a word from their lord to avenge the insult done to him by his ungrateful guest.

Mason clapped his pudgy hands. The sound was moist, tasting of fear. "My men shall provide music for us."

The small band of men who'd followed him into the hall now clustered in front of the closed doors and pulled out various pipes and drums. To Portia's fascination, they began to play.

What came out couldn't be called music. No, it sounded like two tomcats fighting over a she-cat screaming in heat.

She wanted to laugh, or cover her ears as many of her father's men were doing, but she could not. No, she sat like the lady Mason said she was not, and presided over the meal with the composure of a queen. Pretending the caterwauling was as pleasant to her ears as it apparently was to Mason.

Food came and went from the kitchen, and Portia began to grow drowsy. Too much wine, she suspected, but it was too late to do anything about that now.

Mason rose to his unsteady feet. "Now, where is this bed you promised me? Little more than a straw pallet, I suspect, but King Donald will change all that in time!"

King Donald would change nothing at the islands, Portia swore, then rejoiced as the pipers finally finished. The silence was...heavenly.

Except that it wasn't silent. There was the clink of metal, the thump of boots, the...

Someone threw the doors open. "My lord!" the man gasped.

"What is it, man?" Angus asked.

"A...an army! Albans, by the look of them. The yard is full of them. Men and horses!"

Mason seemed smug. "You offered King Donald's envoy your hospitality, Angus. You didn't think I'd be fool enough to come alone, did you? The rest of the envoy waited for their horses to be brought ashore. Some of them may have to sleep in the fields, for now, until we can build barracks for them."

"Get into the barracks with your men. Now!" Angus hissed before he rose and forced a smile. "Of course, Lord Mason. I wish I had known how many guests you'd brought. I fear our paltry feast tonight will not feed so many."

Portia let Grieve hustle her through the kitchens to the barracks, her men falling in behind them. "You, get her things. You, clear mine out and find me a bed in the barracks hall. You and you, you're to stand watch until I tell you otherwise. No one enters the barracks unseen, you hear me?"

His men murmured their assent and divided to do Grieve's bidding.

Portia stared at the barracks hall, a smaller version of the longhouse with beds lined up along the walls. Fires at either end failed to keep away the chill tonight as Portia shivered.

"You will have your cloak soon, my lady," Grieve said. "You shall sleep in the loft, and pull the ladder up after you. Your men will sleep below to keep you from harm."

Portia couldn't seem to form words. Chaos swirled in her head, and she thought she might faint. She drew in a steadying breath, followed by another. "Grieve, tell me true. Is there an Alban army outside, one that outnumbers my father's men?"

Grieve looked into her eyes for a long moment. He had served her for long enough to know not to lie to her. "Are you sure you want to know?" he said finally.

"You could have just said yes," she grumbled. "I want to see them."

"Ascend to the loft. You will see all you need to, my lady."

She hauled her body up the ladder, and soon saw what Grieve meant. The roof that looked so solid from the outside had peepholes along its length, large enough to see through. Or shoot an arrow through, she thought idly.

Men milled around in the yard, and in the fields beyond. Small fires burned on all sides, silhouetting men like monsters from a nightmare.

King Donald had invaded, and she did not know if any of them would survive until morning.

Sixteen

Day dawned, and no one was dead. Except the dozen sheep they'd slaughtered to feed the Albans.

Portia dressed and made her way down the ladder.

"Wait, my lady. We must go with you."

Portia remembered just how many Albans were outside, and decided to do as Grieve said. Cowal and Damhan blocked the doors to the kitchen and outside, anyway. Or they did, until a nod from Grieve had them leading the way out into the yard.

Swallowing, Portia followed.

There were no horses here now, but that meant room for more men. Men who stared with longing and awe.

"That's the girl?"

"Prince Malcolm's bride?"

"Wish I had a wife so pretty."

"Beautiful, isn't she?"

"Wonder why the king doesn't want her himself."

Portia allowed herself a tiny smile at their admiration. It almost soothed away the sting of Mason's insults from last night. He might think her ugly, but he stood alone.

"Make way for milady!" Cowal bellowed, his hand on his sword.

He wasn't the only one. All of them were poised to draw their weapons in her defence. Portia prayed it would not be necessary.

As though they'd heard her silent prayer, the tide of yellow tunics parted, bowing with respect that did not appear feigned. She straightened her spine and marched proudly to the hall. When she reached the warmth it offered, she wanted to relax, but she knew she could not. Men crowded in here, too, as thickly as the yard.

"Good morning, Portia," Father said gravely.

"Good morning, Father," she said as she took her accustomed seat. A servant brought her bread and meat and fruit, and she thanked the girl profusely. When Mason curled his lip and made a disgusted sound, Portia turned to him and said, "Good morning, Lord Mason. I trust you slept well."

His response was a wordless glare.

"I wonder how long you will be willing to endure our humble hospitality?" Portia bit into her bread, not expecting an answer.

"Until something more suitable is built," Mason said. "I have sent men scouting for suitable locations already. I don't suppose there's a quarry on this island. Wood and straw, everywhere I look." He eyed the thatched roof as though it had insulted him.

Portia wouldn't have been surprised if it had. Mason definitely deserved it.

"I hope you find what you're looking for soon," she said sweetly.

"The sooner I have a house befitting my station, the sooner I can keep the prince's bride safe, where she will not be a distraction to my men. Angus, is there somewhere you can keep her in the meantime where she will stay out of trouble?" Mason asked.

Portia wanted to tell him that he was the one who'd brought trouble to her island, but her father's quelling glance kept her quiet. Mason wasn't worth wasting her breath.

"Portia, it might be best if you took your meals in your chambers from now on," Father said.

Her chambers? Or did he mean the loft in the barracks?

Grieve seized her plate. "Let me carry that for you, my lady." He motioned for Damhan to take her cup. With Dermot following close behind her, Portia found herself herded through the kitchen and back to the barracks.

By the time the door closed behind Dermot, Portia was so mad she could spit. "Do you mean to hold me prisoner here? Me?"

"Lady Portia, those are Albans out there. Our people honour you as you deserve but those men would carry you off whether you will or no. When they fight battles on their own soil, they expect their wives to follow after them, and collect the valuables off the corpses of those they've slain. If one of those men tries to take you..." Grieve trailed off.

He didn't need to continue. If someone tried to take her, her men would defend her. That would violate the tenuous truce between guests and host, and there would be war. Her men would die. Her father would die. And Portia herself...she swallowed. Whatever happened, she wouldn't like it.

Hiding in a loft was a small price to pay for her freedom, and her life. Even if her freedom was restricted to a smoky loft above a room where ten men slept and snored and occasionally forgot there was a lady listening.

"I will bring you anything you ask for, as long as you stay safe, my lady," Grieve pleaded. "As long as we have you, Donald cannot conquer Isla."

If only he could bring her Rudolf. She could endure anything, if he were here.

"If you swear to bring me news of

everything that goes on outside these walls…" When she saw Grieve nod, Portia bowed her head. "Then I surrender myself to your care, Grieve."

Seventeen

Rudolf woke to someone trying to yank his head off.

"One, two, three, pull!"

No, make that two someones.

"Stop, you hellspawn whoresons! You'll pull my head clean off my shoulders!" he roared.

"Will you listen to that? He's not dead, after all. The king will be pleased."

Rudolf couldn't see through his helm any more, so he reached up to take it off. The steel wouldn't budge. A careful examination revealed a sizeable dent that ran from his eye to his mouth. If he hadn't worn a helm the blow would have killed him.

"Right, let's try this again. You pull, and I'll try to manoeuvre it so that it actually comes off without taking my head off, too," Rudolf said.

An eternity of tugging, face-pulling and swearing later, a third man joined in the fray, shoving down Rudolf's shoulders as the other two men pulled the helm up.

"Fucking…whoresons…rot in hell!" Rudolf shouted as the steel ripped off his nose, or at least that's what it felt like. When he dared to feel his face, he found his nose still attached, but badly broken. "Thank you. I hope you get your hats stuck on some day so that I might return the favour."

They all laughed, including Rudolf. Because that's what you did if you survived a battle against the odds.

Then a healer came over with a cloth he pressed to Rudolf's already tortured nose. "Fuck off!" Rudolf mumbled through the cloth, but the healer took no notice.

Reidar's wound was tended to, Rudolf

noticed with satisfaction as the king sat down beside him. Reidar still looked like something troubled him, though – something that made him send the healer away.

That got Rudolf's attention.

Reidar dropped his voice so low that only Rudolf would hear the words. "Why did you do that? Call the men to me during the battle?"

Because he needed the help and he was busy, Rudolf wanted to say, but that made Reidar sound weak. Angus would not have questioned it. Harald had been a fool for not teaching his son the most basic things about kingship. "By Lucifer's leathery balls, man! Because it's a man's duty to protect his king. We're yours to command. There's no doubt in anyone's mind that you can fight as well as any man here, and none of us question your right to rule." He tried to smile to lighten his words. "But if you fall in battle, I'll have to sit on your seat, and Aunt Regina will never forgive me."

"What, you don't want a crown, cousin?"

Rudolf's head throbbed at the thought. "Right now, I want nothing on my head at all. My ears are still ringing from the blow to my helm. I would much rather a cup of ale than a crown." And Portia's hands carrying the cup.

Reidar's face clouded, then he turned away from Rudolf as he called for ale.

It took a moment for Rudolf to realise what caused the cloud – suspicion. Regina's poison had truly taken hold in Reidar, and he would never be the king he needed to be while he clung to the lacings of his mother's gown. Reidar belonged on his fucking throne while Rudolf dealt with the borderlands, and it was time the man saw that. To damnation with suspicion and jealousy and playing politics. They spoke plain in the Southern Isles and Rudolf refused to dance around the truth any longer.

Rudolf seized Reidar's arm and pulled him close so that no one might hear his words. "If you die without an heir, your crown falls to me anyway. We both know this. Go back to your castle, get yourself a bride, and put a boy in her belly. Several, if you can. Let me lead the army in your stead."

Reidar raised hopeful eyes to meet Rudolf's. "To what end, cousin? You have a plan, I am sure of it."

Harald had needed Varg, as much as Reidar needed Rudolf now. Rudolf cursed inwardly. Portia would have to wait. "All men plan, but not all plans bear fruit. Rest assured, mine do not need you to die here on a battlefield like my father and yours. I want this kingdom secure as much as you do. These raiders and would-be usurpers must die!" Rudolf raised a fist and shook it, as much at the Opplanders as at the Albans keeping him from Portia.

Reidar regarded him for a long moment before he nodded slowly. "Very well. Will the men follow you?"

Rudolf laughed. "They did today. They're loyal men who serve their king. Why would they not?" Angus would not have doubted him. But then Angus knew him, as Reidar did not. The sooner Reidar left, the sooner he could take command of this army and scour the borders of men who thought the King of Viken was weak. The sooner he was victorious, the sooner he could ask to return to Isla with an army to drive Donald from her shores forever.

Eighteen

News trickled in slower than the rain leaked in through the thatch above Portia's bed. Oh, she'd moved the bed and set a pot beneath the leak, but it hadn't helped speed up the messengers bringing word to Angus about what had befallen the rest of the Southern Isles.

Befallen was the right word, all right. Most of the isles had fallen, much as Isla had. Islanders were hospitable folk, after all. There were exceptions, of course. Lord Calum had taken umbrage at his envoy's demand to hand over his daughter to be the man's bedwarmer, and slain the man on the spot. Dermot had lost two brothers in the ensuing brawl, but Lord Calum still lived, albeit under the heel of an Alban boot. They'd heard no word about his sister, Bedelia, except that she was being held hostage to Calum's good behaviour.

Much like Mason held her here, Portia thought but did not say. Her men knew better than to mention her captivity, and Dermot hastened to continue his report.

"Lord Lewis alone holds out against the invaders," he announced, with a nod to Grieve. "A contrary sea delayed the invaders' ship, so the rider Lord Harris sent from Orken Isle reached him in time to warn him of the treachery of Donald's envoy. Mahon met them with a storm of fire arrows, as though they were the Viken raiders they hate so much. Some still made it ashore, though, and now it is war on Myroy Isle. Lord Lewis has disappeared, leaving Mahon in his stead, intent on killing as many Albans as he can."

Mahon was promised to Bedelia, Portia remembered. She hadn't realised it was a love match until now, but there was naught she could do about it. War parted too many. Grieve and Rhona, Bedelia and Mahon, her and Rudolf…

"Is there any word from the Viken king?" she blurted out.

Surely Rudolf would return if there was.

"None, my lady. Or none that we have heard, anyway," Grieve said. "Mason has been absent much these last few months, though I hear he is still on Isla. Building somewhere suitable to keep a princess, or so he says. Any man with experience in working stone has been called to help with this edifice the man insists on building. He'd been bringing men from the other islands, too, which is why we have so much news to share now."

"Any news of Rum Isle?" Portia ventured.

Her men exchanged uneasy glances. There was news, but it was not good, Portia guessed.

Yet Grieve grinned. "Lord Ronin's longhouse was burned to the ground with no survivors, 'tis said, and the Albans have left the isle entirely, for there is little left on the barren rock." When the others stared at him, he added, "My Rhona is a witch, gifted with fire. Nothing burns on that isle that is not under her power. A blaze that could destroy her father's turf longhouse has to be her doing. My lady lives."

Portia wished she had his confidence about Rudolf. At least they had something to celebrate. "Fetch some wine, then. We shall toast the health and courage of Lady Rhona, Lord Lewis and all who still fight."

Wine was brought and poured. Portia raised a cup with the rest, not having to feign her smile, for any good news was worth celebrating.

"What good tidings have you heard that I have not?"

Her men scrambled to their feet, wine spilling as they remembered to bow to Lord Angus.

"We drink to the courage of Lords Ronin, Calum and Lewis, and their families," Portia said, her eyes daring him to object as she drained her cup.

Angus sighed. "Leave us, please. But do not go far."

Grieve did not hesitate. "Heber, Brian, Dermot – stand guard. The rest of you, archery practice."

"What does the winner get this time?" Berrach asked.

"The chance of victory against Lady Portia in a game of chess this evening." Grieve waited for Portia's nod before continuing, "And remember she can see you from the loft. Let's show her we can defend her even when she cannot practise with us!"

Portia gritted her teeth in what she hoped was an encouraging smile as the men left. Sometimes they set up a target for her in the barracks hall, but it wasn't the same as testing the breeze to see if it would speed or hinder an arrow toward its target. She couldn't remember the last time she'd felt rain on her face. Too long.

"You know if Mason hears you, there will be trouble," Angus began. "It is not politic to wish a guest's enemies well, while he still dwells under your roof."

"Turf him out, then, and tell him that he and his army are no longer welcome here,"

Portia challenged.

He sighed again. "You know I cannot."

That she did, though neither of them liked it.

"Portia, I must leave you for a little while. King Donald has commanded me to provide men to fight the Normans on his southern border, and I must obey." Angus's eyes refused to meet hers.

"Why, Father? What right has he to command you in anything? You are the High Lord of the Southern Isles!"

"If I do not, Mason will take you to Alba."

Portia began, "My men will not allow him to —"

"Your men will be slaughtered. He has an army, Portia, while you have only ten good men. Men who will die to protect you, and Mason will still win. To preserve their lives and yours, I must go."

Portia fought back the building tears. "But what will stop him from doing that if you are gone?"

"He has sworn an oath that he will hold you safe on Isla until my return. I have seen the fortress he is building, and if any edifice can be considered impregnable, it is that place. Please, Portia. Give him no reason to go back on his word. I know you do not like him – nor do I – but if you cross him, it is not just your life at stake. You hold all of Isla in your hands, and it is time you protect her as your mother did. A day may come when a man will rise to claim the isles as their king, and it will be up to you to judge if he is worthy. While the Albans are here, the council cannot convene, but you can make a choice. Whatever happens, you must survive, for while you live, your claim lives with you."

Tears streamed down Portia's face. She was helpless to stop them, or the tide of fate that washed over her with them. "What if I choose wrong?"

Angus's eyes were hard. "If you marry the wrong man, then your dagger must correct your mistake."

Portia swallowed. "You wish me to take my own life?"

"Heavens, no! Did I not just tell you that you must survive? Portia, if you take a husband who is not worthy of you or Isla, then you must bury the dagger in his breast, before he can do any more harm. That is why you must choose wisely, when the time comes." He bowed his head. "Even if I am not here, I trust you will make the right choice."

If she knew the answer to that, would she not have made a choice already? No such man existed, except her own father, and he still lived. For now. "Father…"

"You are the heart of Isla, my lady. Your father is right. When the time comes, you must have courage." Grieve stepped into the barracks. He bowed to Father. "Until then, I will protect her with my life, my lord."

Angus inclined his head. "I would expect no less of you. Your father would be proud, son. I hope you have the chance to tell him one day." He wrapped his arms around Portia and kissed the top of her head. "Farewell, Portia, and you keep that heart safe, you hear me?"

All too soon, the Lord of Isla was gone, and Portia fell to her knees, weeping as she had never done before.

"My lady," Grieve said hoarsely.

She wanted to throw her arms around someone, anyone, just so she wouldn't feel alone. But there was no one left here who could fill that emptiness inside. Rudolf, her father, even her sisters…all gone.

"Leave me," she choked out.

And then she was truly alone, with an unceasing downpour of tears mirrored by the sympathetic sky above. For Isla's heart was broken, and the pieces might never be whole again.

Nineteen

"We agreed on this. I told you war was coming."

Reidar didn't say anything, but he glared plenty.

"There's no excuse now," Rudolf continued. "Let me return home, with the men you promised. You have your heir. Two, even. And a queen who will no doubt give you more if you ask her."

It was the mention of Queen Sativa that did it. "You have a perverse obsession with my queen!" Reidar snapped.

"Send me away, then, as far from her as you can." Rudolf had told him many times he didn't care for Reidar's wife, but since that one flippant comment the day he met her, Reidar wouldn't believe him. Jealous fool.

"That's what she says, too."

This was new.

"Sativa says we must not concede territory we might need to divide among our sons. Even the islands at the edge of the world."

"She's quite astute, your queen. Did she tell you how many men to send with me, too?" Rudolf fought not to sound mocking, but he wasn't sure he succeeded.

"A large raiding party. Three ships."

Rudolf's eyebrows rose. He'd hoped for one. Three was…unexpected bounty. "Thank you."

"But you may only take volunteers. I won't order any man to die so far from home."

"You don't seem all that concerned about me dying," Rudolf said.

"I'm not ordering you anywhere. If you weren't such a stubborn bastard, I'd order you back to the borderlands, but you want to be a hero, to save these islands." Reidar eyed him. "If you can't, I order you to sail right back here so I can tell you I told you so."

"I will not fail," Rudolf said coldly. "I've fought more giants than I can count, protecting your borders. Albans will seem like mere children in comparison."

Reidar grinned. "If the Albans are so soft and tiny, there would be no need for you to go back, then, would there? The Southern Islanders would have defeated them already."

That was what worried Rudolf most. They should have. Unless the Albans had tried some trickery that the Islanders hadn't seen until it was too late. Surely Angus or Lewis...

"You did not see them. Like men who have been at sea too long, their arms and legs like sticks. Driven away from their own land. They weren't fighting men, Reidar. These were Vikens who'd settled on Isla to farm it. Fishermen, farmers, wives, children. Slaughtered, and their village burned to the ground. Those who made it to the boats and arrived here may as well have been ghosts." Rudolf shook his head, but the images would not leave him. "A foreign king has laid claim to our land, and killed our people. I will not endure it on our northern borders, and I will fight it in the southern reaches, too!"

"Like Sativa when we found her." Reidar bowed his head.

Only now did Rudolf realise why the king had refused to see the refugees, though he had not refused them anything else. Sativa had been captured by pirates on her way to marry Reidar, and Rudolf had seen her the day she arrived in Viken. With her torn, bloodied clothes barely covering her emaciated body, Sativa could have been one of the refugees on that fishing boat.

Rudolf had spoken to them all – every man, woman and child. In between slurps of stew from the king's own table, they'd told him what they knew of the situation on the Southern Isles.

The Albans had conquered them. How, they did not know. It seemed the lords had come to some sort of agreement with them almost overnight. Even Angus, though Rudolf did not want to believe it. Angus could not have known about the attack on their village, they'd said, for he was off fighting some foreign war on Alban soil.

"And Lady Portia?" he'd asked, not wanting to know the answer.

Vanished, he was told. No one had seen her since the Albans arrived. She'd last been seen at her father's longhouse, with the young lordlings who were never far from her. They were still at the longhouse – they hadn't gone to war with Angus, which was strange. They did archery training in the mornings, for all to see, Alban army or no. But there was no woman among them.

"Portia is still there on Isla. I know it," Rudolf said, more to himself than his king. "If it were Sativa, would you rest before you had rescued her?"

"I sent our ships out to find her. East, west, north, south...I searched everywhere. And if she had not come to me, I would be searching still," Reidar said. He seemed to see Rudolf clearly for the first time. "Will three ships be enough?"

"I do not know, and I will not until we get

there. Some said the Albans had conquered all of the islands, while others said some still held out. Myroy, Rum…I would have thought Isla, too, and if there is still fighting there, that is where I will go first. If the Islanders know I am there to help, that I come in your name, surely they will join with me to drive out the invaders." Rudolf could not allow himself to believe otherwise. Angus and Lewis were honourable men. They would not have sent him to Viken to beg for help from Harald and now Reidar if they'd meant to ally themselves with Alba.

"I still owe you a barrel of ale I promised you from my wedding," Reidar mused. "I'll send it for your wedding instead. Do you love the girl, Rudolf?"

Rudolf didn't hesitate. "Yes. I've thought of nothing else since I left. Every other woman I've seen only makes me think of her. Even the queen."

Reidar seemed to have forgotten his earlier jealousy. "Do they look so alike?"

Rudolf laughed. "Your queen is like a statue made of gold and ivory, a goddess our ancestors might have worshipped in the old faith. Portia…is a mighty blaze wrapped in lambs' wool. All that passion and power, trapped in a person as soft as goose down. If she were a man, she would be a warrior so mighty even I would fear her. But she is a woman, and all I want to do is stoke that blaze, feed it and protect it until she's willing to engulf me with that roaring passion."

Reidar looked faintly nauseated. "What you dream about in your bed at night is not the sort of thing you tell your king."

Rudolf shrugged. "You asked, my king." He rose. "May I go and recruit some volunteers? I have three ships to fill, and the sooner it is done, the sooner I can be back in my bed, dreaming about the girl I plan to marry."

"Away with you, then!" Reidar sounded stern, but his smile betrayed him. "And don't sail off the edge of the world with those ships, either. I want them back!" he called after Rudolf.

Rudolf made a rude hand gesture and kept going. Not even Reidar would stop him now.

Twenty

When Isla rose out of the mist, Rudolf let out a warcry from the bow of the *Sea Wolf*. His men took it up, echoed by those on the *Sea Dragon* and the *Sea Lion*. The sound had one purpose: to strike fear into the hearts of Viken's enemies. His enemies.

They veered around the cliffs, headed for Portnahaven, the harbour nearest Lord Angus's seat. Nearest Portia, Rudolf promised himself.

He waved at the watch tower on the headland, but no one waved back. He could feel the eyes on him, though. Angus was not fool enough to leave that tower empty.

The pale, rocky sand stretched out on either side, offering him a true Isla embrace to welcome him home.

This was home.

A strange glow appeared in the fog. A glow that spread along the beach like a trail of witchlights in the mist. But witchlights were white.

"Fire arrows!" Rudolf bellowed, but the warning came too late.

The first flaming missile took Sture in the chest, toppling him overboard. Yrian let out an impressive string of expletives, and his men started rowing the *Sea Lion* away from Isla instead of toward it.

A volley of arrows peppered the *Sea Dragon's* sail, scorching the wool that was fortunately too wet to burn.

Frey ordered the *Sea Wolf* to retreat, for Rudolf was too shocked to say anything. The men of Isla knew his warcry. They'd fought beside him often enough in the past. Had they all forgotten him? He hadn't been away that long.

When he'd managed to recollect his wits, Rudolf ordered his men to sail to two other landing spots on the island, but the fog had lifted by the time they reached Macherie, revealing the row of archers waiting for them to come into range. The third landing place was at Kildalton, where the Viken refugees had come from.

Where a thriving town had once stood, now there was nothing but scorched ground, surrounding the stone church and cross that the invaders hadn't been able to burn.

But behind the blackness was a sea of tents. An army camped here, and a shout from their man on watch soon had them lining up archers, ready to shoot Rudolf and his men.

Despair descended on Rudolf as it never had before. To be so close to Portia, and not even be able to land on Isla? Fate was a cruel bitch.

"My prince, what about Myroy?" Frey asked. "There were no archers there when we passed."

The man was right. Lord Lewis ruled

Myroy, or he had, and he had been a friend to Rudolf for the little time he'd known him. He might have news about Portia, and what awaited them on the other islands.

"Set a course for Myroy Isle," Rudolf said.

He'd return to Isla, and next time, he wouldn't leave until the whole island was his, Rudolf swore.

Twenty-One

While his men stayed offshore, Rudolf rowed a fishing boat he'd borrowed into Uig. Lord Lewis had waxed lyrical about the mead in the Uig tavern, and it seemed like the most logical place to ask for information on Myroy Isle.

No archers arrived to greet him. He'd changed from Viken furs to Isla wool, so no one gave him a second glance as he strode up the beach into the town. The tavern was right where Lewis had said it would be, though nowhere near as full. Only something terrible could keep men from drinking. And Rudolf was here to learn what.

He ordered a jug of mead, and paid with coin he hadn't used since he'd left Isla. For a moment, he wished Lewis was here to share the drink like he'd promised he one day would. One day would come, when the war was over, Rudolf swore.

"Is it always so quiet here?" Rudolf asked the tavern keeper.

The man jerked his chin at the jug. "Once you've tasted that, you'll be singing soon enough."

Rudolf hastened to pour himself a drink and compliment the man on it, though Rudolf never tasted a drop. "I mean, I heard word in port that something terrible had happened in the Southern Isles. Some said there was war."

"When there's war, things get burned and men die. Do you see any dying men here?" The tavern keeper peered into Rudolf's face. "I didn't catch your name."

"Rudolf," he offered, pouring a second cup of mead. "Lately come from – "

"Wulf, you're finally here! I thought you'd never come, and I'd die waiting!" an elderly voice cackled, as a heavy hand with the weight of the world behind it thumped down on Rudolf's shoulder. "Get my friend Wulf another jug, for he's promised me a battle!" The smell of strong spirits engulfed Rudolf as the oldtimer gave his cheek a sloppy kiss.

The man kept up a monologue that sounded more nonsense than words, never letting go of Rudolf, until he had the second jug of mead in his hand. His grip turned to steel as his words became clear. "Come, Wulf, I have your oath!" Surprisingly strong fingers dug into Rudolf's shoulder as he was all but dragged outside by the oldtimer.

"This way, Wulf!"

Back to the beach, then along the shore until the fishing boats retreated behind a tumble of rocks. Still the oldtimer led him on.

"Did you bring your chess set, Wulf?" Blue eyes seemed to see into his soul.

How did this oldtimer know? "I did," Rudolf admitted, extracting the board from the bag of belongings he'd brought along. A couple of spare tunics, and his chess set.

The oldtimer's hands set up the pieces with

an easy familiarity Rudolf recognised.

"Now, shall we play, boy?" the man demanded.

"Lord Lewis – " Rudolf began, not daring to believe he was right until the man confirmed it.

"Hush, Wulf. You're here to play, not tell tales about better men than you or me! The birds in the trees have ears, you know." He tried to tap his nose and missed. On purpose, Rudolf suspected.

Rudolf lost three games in quick succession before Lewis held his hand up. "They're gone, I think," he said. "And you have been wasting time in Viken, instead of practising strategy. I'm disappointed in you, Rudolf."

"I was busy fighting real battles for my king, instead of pretend ones where nobody dies, Lord Lewis."

Lewis shrugged. "Harald did fine without you for all these years. Why did he have such need of you now? Did you not tell him about the Albans?" He made the first move.

Rudolf shoved his own pawn forward. "Harald has need of no one any more. His son, my cousin, sits on the throne now, to the annoyance of all his neighbours, who feel his lands and crown belong to them instead." He studied Lewis's second move, and captured his pawn, setting the piece upon the rock beside the chessboard.

"So you have been practising, after all." Lewis regarded the board, and made his move. "Why are you here?"

"To play games with you, it would seem," Rudolf said bitterly, watching Lewis capture his first piece.

"Nay, the game is but the beginning. If you want to capture the queen, you must be ready not just to serve your king, but to become one." Lewis moved his queen into the middle of the board, a move which to an inexperienced eye looked reckless, but Rudolf knew it was anything but.

"Does she still live, Lewis?" He moved his knight to where he might tempt the queen.

"Angus believes so, or he would be home by now. Much like my son, who is one of the young men assigned as Portia's personal guard. If she's still on Isla, as I believe her to be, you'll need an army to free her. Do you have an army yet, son?"

Rudolf's knight claimed another pawn. "I have three ships full of men, but it is not enough," he admitted. "I need more than men, or ships."

"Aye, you're right. You need allies. Powerful ones." Lewis gleefully captured the knight. "Your king's in danger, son."

A rabbit exploded out of the underbrush, flew along the beach and scrambled under a rock, where it sat, quivering.

"Let's go for a walk, Wulf," Lewis said loudly, seizing Rudolf's arm with one hand and the full mead jug with the other. "My old legs get tired, sitting for so long."

Their listeners had returned, Rudolf guessed.

He feigned drunkenness alongside the suddenly unsteady old man, as they made their way along the water's edge. Lewis let out a few scraps of song, slurring the words, before changing to another tune that he murdered as well.

"Which is your boat?" Lewis whispered.

Rudolf led the way, and Lewis leaped

aboard. He shoved the boat into the water and was well out of bowshot before anyone could reach them.

"I hope you weren't lying about that ship, son," Lewis said. "You'll have allies aplenty if you can free them of the Alban curse. The Albans have guest right, and most of our lords are still honour bound to defend them."

So that's how they'd done it. Taking over the islands in a night would have required a lot of coordination. Perhaps Donald was not as stupid as they'd thought.

"Is there anyone I can ask?" Rudolf said.

"Well, there's me, but all I can give you are men, and supplies. If you want to win, what you need is a witch."

"I thought all the witches on the islands had died out," Rudolf said. From what he'd heard, it had been no loss. Some of them had enjoyed the evil they wrought.

Lewis laid a finger beside his nose. No missing it this time. "That's just what they want you to think."

The ships came into view, and Lewis's smile widened. "Oh, you've done well. This new king must like you. When I was a boy, I'd have said three Viken longships could conquer the world. When this is all over, I hope to be able to say it again."

Twenty-Two

The tiny rock island Rudolf rowed up to looked like nobody lived on it – let alone some powerful witch.

"Are you sure this is the place?" Rudolf grumbled, forcing his frustration into each stroke of his oars.

"Absolutely," Lewis replied, settling contentedly in his seat. Of course he was content. He didn't have to row.

"How do you intend to find your witch?"

"No need, son. She will find us. Unless I miss my guess, she already knows we are here.

The real challenge will be persuading her not to set fire to our boots. Or the boat." Lewis eyed the gunwales. "I hope you can swim."

Cursing Lewis for a fool, nevertheless Rudolf brought the boat up to shore and beached it. He waited for Lewis to climb out before dragging the coracle up beyond the high tide line. This time, his wet boots might work to his benefit, if the witch was as volatile as Lewis said.

Lewis led the way up the rocks and onto a rise. He cupped his hands to his mouth. "Lady Rhona, I have a proposition for you!" he shouted, turning to repeat his offer to the other three corners of the island.

"I'm already betrothed, and not to that beast of a man." The sharp female voice came from behind them.

Rudolf whirled. The diminutive girl stood on the sand with her hands on her hips.

Lewis gestured for Rudolf to say something.

"I am no beast, lady," Rudolf said gravely. "I am Rudolf Vargssen, Prince of Viken. I have come from my cousin, King Reidar, to cast the Albans out of the Southern Isles."

She sniffed. "Just you and old Lewis here? You have no chance, Prince of Viken. Not without an army that can match the Albans."

"I have three ships." Rudolf pointed.

"Is this the wolf we are waiting for?" Rhona demanded.

Lewis inclined his head. "He is."

She marched around Rudolf, looking him up and down. "What is your stake, Prince of Viken? What do you get out of saving the Southern Isles?"

Rudolf had never feared anyone so much as he did this dark-eyed imp right now. He opened his mouth, but no sound came out of his inexplicably parched throat.

"He wants Lady Portia," Lewis supplied.

Rhona's eyes narrowed. "Lady Portia is no prize, like the women of other lands. She is the Lady of Isla, and if she does not like you, may heaven help you, for no one else will."

Rudolf laughed. "Portia liked me well enough before I left. If she likes me still…well, I guess we shall see. As long as the lady is safe, I will be satisfied."

"She is safe enough. My betrothed guards

her with his life."

"My son has sent word?" Lewis asked eagerly.

Rhona eyed Rudolf, then answered, "When he can. His letters are carried in secret and left in a place only he and I know. The lady lives, and so does he."

"How goes the hiding, Lady Rhona? Are your sisters sick of fish yet?"

Rhona turned her glare on Lewis. "They complain constantly. The sooner this war ends, the better."

"Would you like to help with the war, Lady Rhona?" Rudolf ventured.

She pursed her lips. "My father will not approve."

Lewis laughed. "Old fool. He thinks my son should save you, for what man would follow a hero who got himself saved by a maiden?"

"Something of that sort."

Lewis jerked his head at Rudolf. "We can blame the victory on the Viken. I'm sure he won't mind."

Rudolf stiffened. "I prefer to fight my own battles, but I am not such a fool as to refuse the help of an ally. There are shieldmaidens among my people, Lord Lewis's late mother among them, who fight alongside their men. If you can assist my army…"

"Ha!" Rhona bit her lip, and the bush behind Lewis burst into flame.

He yelped and ran down to the water, but the fire followed him, blistering the very sands to glass until the sea steamed around him. "I told you! This witch can burn anything! With her on your side, you can't help but win!"

Rudolf fell to his knees. "Lady Rhona, I beg you to help me free the Southern Isles from the invaders. I will give you anything you ask."

She tilted her chin downward so that she might regard him. "I want all I've ever wanted. My husband. Free him from his oath to Portia, so that he can come home and marry me." With a wave of her hand, she extinguished the fire and a breeze came out of nowhere to blow away the smoke as though it had never been. "What would you have me burn first?" The fire burned in her eyes now, and it was a terrifying thing.

"Myroy Isle, and every other island where

Albans seek to hide," Lewis said, splashing out of the sea. He shrugged off Rudolf's and Rhona's stares. "What? I'm the Lord of Myroy. I can burn it if I want to." He fumbled around under his cloak and pulled out the jug of mead Rudolf thought he'd left on the shore at Myroy. Lewis uncorked the jug and lifted it in a toast: "To winning this damned war!" He drank deeply.

Rudolf held out his hand to Lady Rhona. "Do we have an accord?"

Her hand seemed so small in his, but the heat in her fingers reminded Rudolf that power came in many forms. "We do, Wolf Prince."

Twenty-Three

Rudolf rowed ashore under cover of darkness. Lewis snorted awake mid-snore as Lady Rhona leaped into the water to help Rudolf drag the boat beyond the waves.

"My lady..." Rudolf began.

"Shut it, Wolf," she snapped. "Your lady's not here. Lewis?"

"We check the houses. See if there's anyone left. Then I alert the tavern." Lewis smiled evilly.

The only lights in Uig were in the tavern, but Rudolf checked anyway. House after house was empty – people and their possessions gone. He met up with Lewis on the road to the beach. "No one left," Rudolf said.

"I found a few hiding, but they only came for supplies. They'll return to the caves tonight." Lewis squared his shoulders. "Are your men ready, do you think?"

Rudolf smiled. "Light the lamp, and you shall see."

Lewis unshuttered his lamp, and an answering light flared to life in the bay.

The sounds of a Viken drinking song floated across the water.

"Hey, I know that one," Lewis said. He seized Rudolf's hand and broke into a run.

"Vikens! In the bay! In ships!" he shouted, repeating his frantic call to arms all the way up the road to the tavern. He staggered through the door, breathlessly announcing, "Vikens in the harbour!" before he collapsed spectacularly on the floor.

Rudolf had to step over Lewis to enter the tavern. "I saw them too," he said. "Invaders!" He didn't need to pretend. Albans were enough to bring a genuine snarl to his face.

The men he'd taken for Islanders earlier in the day rose from their seats and headed outside with grim purpose.

"Vikens! To arms!" The shout from outside issued from more than one mouth.

The barman set out two cups and filled them, then pushed them toward Lewis. Lewis took one, and gestured for Rudolf to take the other.

"Fill one for yourself, man," Lewis commanded, and the barman obeyed. All three men lifted their cups before Lewis continued, "To victory!"

The barman drained his cup, then wiped his mouth on his sleeve. "So it is time, then?"

"Time to fight!" Lewis slammed his empty cup on the counter. "Come on, son. Drink up, or you'll miss it!"

Rudolf did not need to be told twice. Down went the mead, and it was with the memory of sweetness on his tongue that he said, "Leave town now, if you want no part in the battle."

The barman slapped a greatsword on the bar, followed by a bow and a clacking quiver of arrows. "I'm no coward. Lead the way, my lord."

Rudolf returned to the now deserted street. The Alban drinkers had run off for reinforcements and the unmistakeable march of booted feet in the distance heralded their arrival.

Rudolf cupped his hands round his mouth and let out his loudest warcry. A faint answer came from the boat in the bay. The rest of his men were in place, then.

The booted feet quickened their pace and for the first time, Rudolf saw them. As though every Alban he'd ever killed in his boyhood had come back to life, carrying torches as they raced to take their revenge. But not tonight. No, tonight they passed him by, headed for the beach.

The Albans formed up along the shore, lifting bows and nocking arrows. Runners made haste along the lines, carrying buckets of oil and torches to set the fire arrows alight.

In the bay, the *Sea Wolf*'s sodden crew struck up a tune again, louder this time. They paddled parallel to the shore, still singing.

"Fire!" someone shouted, and the arrows

flew. Arcing across the water to shoot the waves, sending up puffs of steam before they sank.

"Again!"

More arrows flew, but the boat was out of range.

Frey rose from his seat and bellowed, "The shore's that way, you fools! Turn this boat around!"

The singing men proceeded to row the boat in a circle, following the curve of the bay. Arrows rose and fell, but didn't hit their mark.

"Cease fire!" The Alban commander had seen sense. "Wait until they are in range!"

But Frey was not as drunk as he seemed, and every man aboard the *Sea Wolf* knew to keep their distance, however loudly they sang.

While Frey kept the Albans distracted, the rest of the Vikens crept out of the dunes. All of the raiders were veterans who'd fought the Opplanders under Rudolf's command – the enemy would not know they were there until they wanted them to. And then, it would be too late.

Rudolf silently signalled where he wanted

his men. When they were in place, he let out another warcry.

"Vikens in the town!" came the shout from the beach.

Arrows rained down on the houses, setting fire to roofs and walls alike. Vikens poured from the houses and into the street, running from the town as though fleeing from the fire.

The Albans gave chase, only to find the way blocked by a hay wagon that hadn't been there on their march in.

Rhona freed the horse from the wagon, gave it a slap on the rump to send it away, and stared at the wagon. The hay blazed into life.

The Alban soldiers turned to go back the way they'd come.

Only to find the way blocked by another wagon, driven by Lewis. Rhona cast some spell and set that alight, too.

Panicked soldiers turned to the houses, only to be met by a hail of arrows from both sides.

Rudolf climbed atop the tavern's roof – the only one not burning, for fire arrows didn't work on sod – and set his own bow to work. Beside him, the tavern keeper proved to be a surprisingly good shot.

In the flickering orange light, Rudolf glimpsed hell – dead and dying men, crawling and crying for help that would not come. Albans, all, as his men abandoned the burning houses to climb on the roof beside him.

Men still milled around on the beach – Albans who hadn't managed to get into the town before it went up in flames. Rudolf lifted his bow to finish the job.

A hand shot out and grabbed his bow. "Nay, let them run," Lewis said softly. "Rhona can speed them on their way. They have a tale to tell."

Ribbons of flame snaked across the sand, biting at the boots of the Albans who remained on the beach. "Run, ye cowards!" she screamed. "The Wolf Prince is coming for you, and all your kind! The Wolf Prince will burn out every Alban until the Southern Isles are free of you!"

The men swarmed over the fishing boats, launching a frightened flotilla into the bay as the *Sea Wolf* beached itself on shore.

"Shall we go after them, sir?" Frey shouted.

Rudolf shook his head. He watched the boats drift away, reminding himself that each battle brought him closer to Portia. To home.

"The war has begun," Rudolf said.

Lewis slapped him on the back. "And we'll need more mead before it's done. Padraig, get our Viken brothers a drink!"

"Yes, my lord," Padraig the barman said.

Twenty-Four

Portia watched the Albans pack their things onto their horses and head for Portnahaven, casting frightened looks around them as they went.

"Where are they going?" she asked.

"Some say to fight the Normans back in Alba, while others say they're being sent to fight the Wolf." Grieve shrugged and rubbed at a stubborn spot on his armour. "The lot of them pray that they might be sent home, for they've found a cold welcome here."

"I hope they're being sent to the Wolf, and

he kills the lot of them," Portia said.

Tales of the Viken prince had reached her even here, for with Mason gone, her men shared meals and news with the Albans. News they were only too happy to bring back to her.

"They are fighting men, no different from us, truly," Dermot piped up. "And I wouldn't wish the Wolf on any man. They say he moves like a ghost, taking a town before anyone knows he is there. And he burns places to the ground, with all the people inside, too. 'Tis a terrible death, to be burned alive."

Portia paled. "Towns? You mean the Viken prince can't tell the difference between our people and Albans?"

"Perhaps. It's not like the Wolf has lived among us, my lady," Grieve said. "Or mayhap he does not care. Our people gave the Albans shelter, invited them onto land the Viken king claims. While they dwell in our halls, we must defend them, too. If he sees us as Alban allies against him, you cannot blame a man for calling us all his enemies."

"I have not taken up arms against him! Neither have you." Portia smoothed her skirt to hide her consternation. "Surely he will not consider us his enemies."

"But we will take up arms against him, my lady. We are all honour bound to defend you. We swore an oath."

She remembered. How could she not? But the thought that these men, her only friends, would be forced to die for her, was one she was not willing to face.

"Why do they call him the Wolf?" she asked. "Surely the prince has a name."

"He has many names, lady," said Damhan. "The Wolf, or the Wolf Prince. Lately, the one I hear most from the Albans is the Big, Bad Wolf." He laughed. "He sounds like a villain from a children's tale, but he frightens grown men as well as children."

"Why?" Portia persisted.

"He's a Viken giant, as big as they come," Brian said. "Any man who burns whole villages cannot be good. They say he torched the port at Myroy when he first landed, and every town he's touched since. And he is as crafty as a wolf. The Albans who fled Myroy said they would see one Viken and hurry to attack, only to find themselves surrounded and outnumbered. He has a mighty army, all giants like him, and he will not stop until the Southern Isles are his."

A man so mighty, even the Albans fled from him. And all Portia had to protect her were ten good men. She shivered. "What does he do to the women he captures?"

"He's a Viken, so 'tis not hard to guess," Brian said. "Rapes 'em, takes the pretty ones to his ship to be whores back in Viken, and kills the rest."

"Brian!" Grieve roared. "Have you forgotten who you're speaking to?"

Brian shrugged his meaty shoulders. "Sorry if I offended, Lady Portia, but you did ask."

She had, though she wished she hadn't. Her people had allied with the Vikens to stop them from such things, but it was all for naught if this Big, Bad Wolf saw fit to ignore that and enslave them all instead.

"Set up my target for me. I wish to practise archery again, so that when I see this Wolf, I can shoot him," Portia said.

Cowal grinned and rose. "I shall do it, my

lady. If you shoot the Wolf, I want to watch."

Twenty-Five

Isla rose from the ocean, naked in the sun. Waiting for him. Rudolf's heart swelled within his chest.

No archers stood on the shore this time, and his three ships led a veritable flight of dragon boats from every inhabited island in the Southern Isles. They were filled with men from all the isles, too, not just those from Viken. Isla was ever the heart of the isles, and they would not be free of the Albans until they had been driven from Isla's shores.

Rudolf saluted the watch tower as they

passed, wondering if they had sent a runner with word to wherever the remaining Alban army lurked. It mattered not. He and his men knew every landing spot on Isla, and they would not be driven off this time. They would land, and they would fight, until they won. Isla would be his.

The sand crunched beneath his boots, and Rudolf almost wept. Home. He was home. Movement in the watch tower above caught his eye, and he turned to squint at the cliffs. A flash of red or orange, maybe, on the heights? If he looked closely at the window just beneath the thick straw thatch, he could almost see it.

He grabbed Frey, whose eyes were better than his. "Look at the watch tower, and tell me what you see," Rudolf commanded.

Frey shaded his eyes. "I see…an archer. Maybe more than one. Would you like me to take some men to flush them out, sir?"

Portia. His mind flew to her, though he knew it could not be. Portia would not be atop some tower, waiting to shoot men coming ashore. She would be with her men, who would protect her.

Unless this eyrie was the best place to keep her safe. Two archers could hold the cliff path for a long time.

"Pick two, and follow me," Rudolf said, setting off up that very path. He huffed and puffed a little, for it was steeper than he remembered. He knew when he was within bowshot, for he'd manned the tower himself for Lord Angus. Only then did he tug his helm down over his head and take his shield off his back. The familiar weight on his arm reminded him of the borderlands – the last place he'd needed it. He'd fought no open battles since he left Viken. On Isla, though, that would change. Everyone said this was where the Alban leader lived, and where else would his army have retreated to?

Peering over his shield, Rudolf definitely saw something orange at the top of the tower. Orange, and moving. He took a deep breath, followed by another, but there was smoke in the air. Not fire, then.

Three strides up the path, he heard the whistle of an arrow. Up came his shield, but the missile fell short, slicing into the turf several yards ahead. He darted forward to retrieve it, then skipped back out of range before he dared to examine the arrow. An arrow from Isla, not Alba – he'd recognise the feathers in the fletching anywhere.

More arrows flew, bouncing off rocks and the path ahead.

"You'll not have Isla while I live and breathe, oathbreaker!" a female voice shrieked as a fist shook out of a window, high above.

Rudolf laughed.

"What would you have us do, sir?" Frey asked, bringing Alf and Erik up the path with him.

Rudolf blew out an exasperated breath and pointed at the tiny fist. "Fetch her down, and anyone hiding up there with her. Tell her if she doesn't come, I will bring the whole tower down around her."

Alf grinned. "Gladly, sir."

Rudolf held up his hands. "Without hurting her. She's to be brought to me, unharmed."

His men dashed inside. He waited, knowing they'd reached the top when shrieked curses cascaded down. He wasn't sure who was the whoreson or the walrus's...tail-warmer, but he filed the insults away for a later date. They would keep.

Slowly, the shrieking descended. The men let out cries of pain as the valiant lady fought back, and Rudolf almost regretted not allowing them to defend themselves. It was their own fault for not going into battle with full armour, he decided, feeling a smile lift his lips as the lady's boots came into view. Boots, and the most enormous belly he'd ever seen.

It took both Alf and Erik to hold her arms while Frey brought up the rear, keeping her upright so as not to damage the baby she carried.

Rudolf couldn't seem to close his mouth. Portia, heavily pregnant? To who?

"If you've torn my dress, you whoresons, I'll see you sew it back together yourselves!" she threatened. Her blazing eyes turned to Rudolf, who was glad his helm protected him from her wrath. "And you! A misbegotten wolf who has broken every oath the Vikens have sworn to us! Conquering your allies – your friends! You are no friend of mine, you...you...dog!" She even tried to spit at him, but Angus's daughters were too well-bred to manage such a feat.

Not Portia. He should have known from her poor aim. Arlie couldn't shoot a target a yard in front of her. Portia would have pinned the toes of his boots to the path before turning him into a pincushion.

Rudolf swallowed back his disappointment. Arlie would know where Portia was. Though not Portia herself, her sister was the next best thing. "Take her to Rhona," he said.

Not all of his men could be trusted around a pretty woman, even a pregnant one, but they kept a goodly distance from Rhona, and rightly so. She'd burned a few boots before they'd learned.

Erik and Alf left with the girl, but Frey remained.

"Was there anyone else?" Rudolf asked.

Frey shook his head. "Just her, and this." He held up the bow and quiver. A half-full quiver and a man's bow. What Arlie had been thinking, climbing to the top of the tower in such a state to shoot a bow she hadn't the strength to use, he did not know. But he could ask her that, too.

"Once the men have landed, find somewhere to make camp. Send out scouts, and have them report to me before sundown. Based on their information, we move out in the morning," Rudolf said.

"Yes, sir."

He supervised camp construction, breaking up more than a dozen fights that erupted before the men were settled. They might all oppose the same enemy, but they were an independent lot with grievances going back generations that none of them would forget. The men of Vatersay could not abide to be beside the men of Langroy, and the men of Eriska and Grimsay brawled if they so much as spoke to one another. Add those to the general complaints that one man had a better campsite than another, be it bog or rock or soft grass, and the men from Islay would defend their island with fists or weapons, if need be.

When evening fell, he was more exhausted than he'd believed possible. His shoulder ached from intercepting a punch meant for one of the Myroy men, delivered by an Eriskan with fists like hams. But as enticing scents started to waft from well-established cookfires, he knew his day was not over yet. He liberated a small pot of stew, three bowls and some bread, and headed for Rhona's tent. Where he would have to interrogate the prisoner.

Rhona met him outside, as if she knew he was coming. Magic, most like, but it still unnerved him. He'd seen the things she could do and he had to admit she terrified him just as much as she did his men, but he hoped he hid it better.

"I hope you know what you're doing," she greeted him. Rhona jerked her head at the tent. "My business is magic, not midwifery. If she births the babe in there, you'll be the one catching it, not me."

Arlie was in labour, and Rudolf would have to deliver the babe? He couldn't hide his horror. "I'll send someone for a midwife directly," he said, turning to find someone, anyone, he could ask.

Rhona laughed. "She doesn't need one yet. Some months to go, I understand." She eyed the food in his arms. "Did you bring any wine?

Ah, no matter. I heard the Eriskans brought plenty. I shall go and find some, for maybe that will loosen the lady's tongue. She had little to say to me that is not about the babe in her belly." She set off, and the men parted to allow her to pass.

Whoever her betrothed was, he was a lucky man. She paid the other men no heed, unless they became impertinent. Then the smell of burning leather boots would waft across the camp and a healer would be summoned to put salve on the burns.

Rudolf cleared his throat as he poked his hand through the tent flaps. "Are you in a fit state for visitors, my lady?"

Arlie's voice was just as he'd remembered it. "If you're looking for the witch woman, she's gone for dinner. If you're her lover, I suggest you find somewhere else to spend the night. I will not share a tiny tent with some rutting fool she will forget as soon as her true husband returns."

Rudolf stepped inside. "I'm not Lady Rhona's lover, I promise you, Arlie. I came to talk to you."

Arlie's eyes lit up. "Rudolf!" She tried to rise, but instead she just seemed to rock back and forth. "Damn this belly, I feel like a whale. You must come here and give me a kiss!" She held out her arms.

Rudolf kissed her cheek and sat beside her. "I brought dinner. It's not roast pork from your father's kitchens, but it's the best we have."

She took the offered food and ate with the appetite of a woman starving. Rudolf wordlessly handed her his portion as well, and began to worry there would be none left for Rhona.

"Maybe later," Arlie said, setting Rudolf's bowl down. "I am so hungry all the time, and yet if I eat too much, this baby of mine is like to kick a hole right through me. Very defensive of his territory, he is."

"Who is his father?" Rudolf asked. If some Alban had taken liberties with Lord Angus's daughter, he'd kill the man himself.

"Widald the whale hunter," Arlie said, her fond smile telling the tale of her love for her Islander husband. "He spotted a likely bull in the water yesterday, and left with promises to bring me back a whalebone cradle. How could I refuse such a man?"

"But why were you in the watch tower? And why was no one with you?" Rudolf pressed.

Arlie shrugged. "It is the best place to watch for whales, and for whale hunters coming home. The girls from the village come to visit every day, bringing food and word of what is happening. None have visited today, but when I saw this army sailing in, I sat at the window with Widald's old bow to defend my home, as any good Islander wife would when raiders come. The things this Wolf Prince has done..." She shook her head and muttered something about walruses under her breath. "What are you doing with this man and his rabble, Rudolf?"

Rudolf didn't know what to say. Telling her he was the leader of what she called rabble didn't seem like the best idea. Evidently she hadn't recognised him as the man she'd shot at, now he'd taken his armour off. Finally, he said, "They may seem disorganised, but they are united in a common purpose. Viken men and men of the Southern Isles fighting the Albans together, as our longstanding alliance says we will do."

She pursed her lips. "Not just fighting the Albans. I've heard the stories, even here. I bet Portia has, too. Whole villages burned, and everyone killed. How could you, Rudolf?" Tears sprang to her eyes. "Women. Children! How could you kill children?"

"I've never killed a child!" Rudolf protested, but he had hazy memories of Opplander boys wielding axes they could scarcely lift. Boys old enough to be at war, who were trying to kill him, however clumsily. He'd been the same age when he first went into battle, and he hadn't shied away from anyone who tried to kill him. As for women…like Vikens, Opplander women fought as fiercely as their men. He had several scars from wounds inflicted by women warriors. "This army has only fought Albans. Well, mostly Albans," he amended, thinking of the brawl he'd broken up only an hour before when a Viken had mistaken a Myroy man's drinking cup for his own. "They are good men, Arlie, I swear to you. They are here not to conquer Isla, but to free it."

"And this Wolf Prince? What sort of man is he?" she challenged. "Why do you follow him, Rudolf?"

She truly did not know he and the Wolf were one and the same, and Rudolf did not want to be the one to enlighten her. If he did, then he would have to tell her the truth – he hadn't come to free Isla, but to free Portia. What manner of man went to war over one woman? It sounded like madness, even to him. Madness that a whole army followed.

"I do not know," he muttered, rising to his feet. Before she could say another word, he'd left the tent to walk the camp perimeter with only his own dark thoughts for company.

Twenty-Six

When day dawned, Rudolf was resolute. He'd managed a second interview with Arlie, where she'd told him the last she'd heard, Portia was still in her father's house. No one had seen her for months, but her personal guard were there, and her men did not hide, so where they were, she would be, too.

It was strange to think of Portia as having multiple men, like she kept a harem of sorts. What did one call a stable of men? A barracks, or a company, perhaps – for they were a military unit, sworn to protect her, and not her lovers.

It took the men half the day to break camp, to Rudolf's bewilderment. If they did not move faster, it would take them three days to reach Angus's house, when it was less than a day's ride. But determination drove him – determination to free Portia and her lands from the enemy, and he needed the army at his back to ensure he did, this time.

Their slow progress gave him time to send out plenty of scouts, and mull thoughtfully on their reports. None of his men had seen a single Alban. In fact, they'd seen few men at all, though the villages on Isla were far from deserted. Women and children eyed the army warily as they passed, some unsheathing daggers they tried to hold in the folds of their skirts, ready to defend what was theirs.

His men knew better than to attack a village without an express command from Rudolf. These were their own people, not their enemies. He made sure to pay for any livestock they took, and the sight of coins loosened tongues that hadn't been free to speak for some time.

The Alban camp had been around Angus's house, though there were rumours of a second to the north, where Mason, the Alban commander, had a castle, or so it was said. Everyone seemed to know someone who had worked on the edifice, but none had seen it, or knew where it was. Somewhere hard to reach, they all agreed, before telling him it was on a clifftop, an island, or in the middle of a lake.

Rudolf found himself imagining an underwater castle, where basking sharks sat on thrones while mermaids serenaded them. Or would it be the other way around? He'd heard tales of a mermaid who married a king, and she now presided over his court, her long gowns hiding her tail and scales from all those who might know her for what she was.

"Sir, the men from Vatersay and Longroy are fighting again. It seems the only land left for them to pitch camp is a bog barely big enough for one of their groups, let alone both, and with no distance between them."

Rudolf swore. They were like brawling children. A pity he could not spank them all. "Send for Lady Rhona," he instructed. "Ask her to dry out the bog. Once she is done, I am sure there will be room for everyone. They will be bedfellows in the bog, or they may sail home."

Yrian grinned. "Yes, sir."

He liked the young witch, Rudolf was certain of it. He didn't seem to fear her as much as the rest, though he kept a healthy distance from her, too. If Rhona's betrothed died before she could marry the man, Rudolf had no doubt Yrian would offer himself in the man's stead.

Rudolf crested the rise and his breath caught in his throat. He knew they'd set up camp on the same site the Albans had deserted, but the sight of Angus's longhouse sent a wave of longing through his body that he wished would carry him to the door and happier times.

His scouts said the place was deserted, but Rudolf knew better. Even if Angus and the Albans had left, someone remained. The house and outbuildings had a watchfulness to them that Rudolf had learned not to ignore.

He wore a breastplate, but not his helm, and

he carried his bow and his quiver on his back. His sword bumped against his side with each step, but he would not need his shield today. Not for this.

The cookfire in the kitchen had burned down to coals, but there was no mistaking the fact that it had been used to prepare a meal today. A basket of apples lay on the table, their leaves not yet withered, as though they'd been picked only hours before. Someone was here. Someone who cooked, and took care to harvest the orchard.

A shrill scream that sounded like a distressed horse came from outside.

Rudolf picked up an apple and went outside to investigate.

The mare, a skittish beast that lifted her tail, threw back her ears and eyed him with menace before letting out a squeal, trotted away from him to rub herself against the fence. She stared him a while longer, as though daring him to try and ride her so that she might buck him off, before heading to the feeding trough to finish off her oats.

The second scream didn't come from her –

it came from the stables. Rudolf hurried to help.

The stables were as empty as the kitchen, except for the screaming horse, doing his best to kick down the door of his stall.

"Hector!" Rudolf lifted the bar to let the stallion out, then held out the apple. Would his horse still recognise him after all this time?

Hector ignored the apple and stepped on Rudolf's foot as he shoved past him to leave the stable.

Rudolf followed him, not willing to lose the beast.

Hector took off at a gallop, soaring over the fence, before landing in the mare's field. He moved purposefully toward her feeding trough.

Rudolf halted. The perverse beast had put himself where Rudolf would have taken him. Perhaps he knew better, and Rudolf should return to the buildings. Reuniting properly with his horse could wait.

He returned to the yard between the longhouse, the kitchen and the stables. Only now did he see the new building, its fresh cut timber splintering his memories of this place. The barracks hall had not been here when he left, and its newness meant it could only have been built by Albans, for who else would construct a wooden barracks where a sod-roofed longhouse would do? The only Islanders who preferred timber were the men of Myroy, who didn't have enough sod for roofs, though they had plenty of trees.

The barracks did not belong, and they would burn, he huffed to himself.

Rudolf reached for his quiver. He stabbed his arrow point into a block of the soft, white, waxy substance that made it burn whatever it touched. He marched into the kitchen and thrust the arrow into the ashes, but the stuff didn't catch. Swearing, he found some pine needles in the box of tinder and threw them among the coals.

A wisp of smoke rose up. Throwing his arrow on the flagstones behind him, Rudolf dropped to his knees and blew the tiniest puff of air at the smoking needles. He held his breath for a moment, watching, praying…and then they caught, flames licking up them as if they wanted to swallow the needles whole.

Again he stuck the arrow in the heart, and this time, the flames gratefully accepted his offering. Rudolf hurried out side with his blazing arrow, knowing he needed to fire the thing before the stuff melted and set fire to the kitchen.

Outside, the sun blinded him for a moment. He turned, glared at the barracks, and let his arrow fly. No need to aim when his target was as big as a house. His arrow arced up and hit the roof, then disappeared, as if by magic. Rudolf's mouth dropped open. What in heaven's name had happened to his arrow?

Smoke curled out of a hole he hadn't seen before. Several holes, actually – arrow slits in the roof, he realised.

"What do you think you're doing, you stupid beast?" a female voice yelled behind him.

Rudolf whirled in time to see a redheaded woman sprint past him, carrying a broom. He followed her around the stable to the field where Hector had...ah.

"Get off her, you randy bastard!" she shouted at Hector, who was too busy servicing the mare to care.

"You're too late, he's probably already got her with foal by now," Rudolf called, more to protect his horse than anything else. He would not want to be interrupted while making love to a lady, though he'd have chosen a more private place than Hector had.

"Did you let that menace out?" The woman rounded on him.

"He would have kicked the door down if I did not," Rudolf said.

She snorted. "You try telling Portia that. Mache is her mare."

"Lina?" he ventured.

"Of course, you fool. Portia would've whacked you with the broom, not the bloody horse. First for being away so long, and then for letting the horse out. Then I think she might've burst into tears." Lina smiled. "What kept you, Rudolf? She's missed you so much."

"I serve at my king's command," he said simply. What more could he say? "Where is she, Lina?"

"If you were here sooner, I could say the loft." Lina pointed at the barracks building.

Her eyes widened. "Why is there smoke?" She hurried toward it.

Rudolf grabbed her to pull her back. "Because it's on fire."

Lina wrenched out of his grasp. "Well, aren't you everybody's hero, then? First you let the horse out, and then you set fire to the barracks. What else have you done? If you bring the army down on this house, I will hit you with this broom."

Rudolf stared down at her eyes, as fierce as Portia's could be. He swallowed. "What if I told you the army is here to free Isla from the Albans?"

"So Keith was right." At Rudolf's blank look, Lina explained, "My husband. He's Father's steward, sending supplies to where he's fighting the Normans. He's seeing to a shipment of salt mutton, or he'd be here. Are you here to free Portia, too?"

From husbands to mutton to Portia, Rudolf wasn't sure if he could keep up. Especially with the barracks definitely on fire now – flames licked at the roof through holes that didn't seem so tiny any more.

"Where is Portia?" Rudolf asked again.

"He's taken her."

"Who?"

Lina sighed. "You've been away too long, Rudolf. Lord Mason, the Alban bastard who tricked Father and the other lords into hosting Donald's armies. He's an arrogant prick who pisses off anyone who hears him, but he works well with stone. He built himself a castle in the north, the sort of thing even the Normans would envy, or so 'tis said. You'll need an army to get in, and maybe not even then. That's where he's taken her."

"Where?"

Lina shrugged. "Some holy spot in the north, where the lords meet and drink so many barrels of ale they empty half our cellars."

"Council Island, on Loch Findlugan?" Rudolf asked, horrified. He didn't want to believe it. The Albans had built on the holiest site in the Southern Isles?

"That's the spot!" The fire crackled loudly behind her, seizing Lina's attention for the first time. "So you really are burning down Portia's barracks, are you? You're lucky she likes you.

Her men built that, and kept her safe in the loft while the army was here. They won't take kindly to you when they see you've destroyed all their hard work."

"Are they with her?" If he could not be with her, at least someone kept her safe until he could be.

"Of course. They are her sworn men. She — " Lina stared. "Who in heaven's name is that ruffian?"

A man staggered up the street, dressed in stained rags. He looked like he'd been buried in a bog and clawed his way out again. "You have to help me!" he shouted. He fell to his knees at Lina's feet. "Don't let the Vikens get me. Don't!" He caught sight of Rudolf and crumpled into a sobbing heap on the ground. He pawed at Lina's boots. "You must do as I say, you ugly whore!" His words ended in a scream as his clothes started to smoke.

Rudolf dragged Lina back from the flames a second time as the man turned into a human torch. Only one person could have done this.

"Rhona!" he shouted.

Rhona strode up the street, looking

supremely unconcerned. "He grabbed me, said some things that were not very complimentary, and tried to order me about. I set fire to his boots, and he ran off, so I thought that was the end of it. So when he did the same to this lady here, I figured he hadn't learned his lesson." She leaned over and spat on his smoking skeleton. "He was Alban, anyway. No loss. Oh, and he dropped this." She held up a large gold medallion, attached to a thick gold chain. "Probably stolen. Albans rob the dead on the battlefield. Keep it as a war trophy."

Rudolf wanted to say something, anything, but he couldn't seem to find the words. He'd killed many a man, but Rhona's cold-blooded slaughter seemed different, somehow. Despite the blaze behind him, he shivered.

Rhona regarded the burning building. "Ah, I'm not the only one who's been setting fires. Nice work, Rudolf. Perhaps you don't need me any more."

"I do," he blurted out. "The Albans have taken Portia to their castle in the north. On Loch Findlugan. The very heart of the isles. I need all the help I can get to free her from them."

Rhona gave him a long look. "I'll honour our agreement, if you'll do the same."

Rudolf bowed his head. "You know you have my word."

Twenty-Seven

Loud hammering startled Portia out of sleep. "What is it?" she mumbled sleepily.

"Stay aloft, my lady," came Grieve's quiet response from below.

She heard the scrape and thunk of someone unbarring the door. "What's amiss?" Berrach rumbled.

"Tis the Wolf. He's landed on Isla, and she must be moved."

Fear trickled down Portia's spine. The Viken prince was here. The man who killed and burned everything in his way. Who would kill her men, burn this building like the woodpile it was, and when he got hold of her…Portia swallowed. Would he care about her claim, or see her as just another woman to rape?

"Seems to me there's more danger on the road than here," Grieve said.

"Perhaps, which is why we must move quickly, and under the cover of darkness. If we reach the castle by dawn, no one will be able to reach her. She will be safe behind my walls, I swear."

Mason. Their visitor was Mason, who sounded as frightened as Portia felt. Good. She hoped the Wolf raped him first, or at least ran him through so she could watch.

"My sister will be here tomorrow. We must wait for her. I cannot leave her for the Wolf," Portia called down.

Grieve tried to hush her, but Portia would not be silenced tonight. She shoved the ladder through the trapdoor and began to climb down. "You hush yourself, Lewisson. If I do not agree to go – "

"Then I will tie you to my saddle and carry you myself," Grieve finished for her. "I'm sorry, my lady, but your safety is more important than your wishes. Or your sister. We shall leave your things in the longhouse with a note for her to send them on. Pack only what you can carry, for if the Wolf is on Isla, then he is within a day's ride of here. We cannot defend you here with so few, but what I've heard of Mason's castle is such that it might be defended by ten men, for it is a formidable place. Dermot will wake the kitchen maids and the cook – they will come, too, for there will be no other women to keep you company otherwise."

Portia wanted to argue, but she knew he was right. So she glared at Grieve instead.

"You've been complaining for months about being a prisoner here, and how you never get to go riding. Don't you want to ride Mache?" Grieve coaxed.

"She's in heat. She'd bite anyone who tries to saddle her. I must leave a note for my sister, telling her not to let Mache get near any of the other horses until she settles. If she hurts Hector, Rudolf will never forgive me."

Grieve's shoulders relaxed. "Thank you, my

lady. It would try me sorely to have to tie you to the saddle like a prisoner."

She smiled grimly. "Sore is right. I'd bite or stab anything I could reach. I'll not be thrown over any man's saddle without a fight."

"Aye, I know."

"Have the men prepare the horses. All but Hector and Mache. They must stay." For a moment, she hesitated. What if the Wolf hurt Hector? If he did, she would tell Rudolf what his countryman had done.

"You pack your things. I will take care of all else," Grieve said.

Back up the ladder Portia went. She bundled up some spare clothes and pulled on some boots. Everything else she owned went into the chest of her mother's that her men had brought from the longhouse for her. She lifted her bow and quiver. "What will happen to the things I leave?" she called down.

"A groom will take the wagon, and follow behind us. Whatever you want him to bring should arrive late on the morrow," Grieve said.

She shouldn't need to shoot anyone between now and then. She'd be inside the castle before it was light enough to see her target, surely. She dropped the bow and quiver in the chest and slammed the lid shut. "I'm coming down. 'Twill just take a moment to pen a note for my sister, and I will be ready." She dropped her cloak and bundle on the barracks floor and launched herself after them.

"My lady!" Grieve lunged forward to catch her.

Portia landed neatly on her feet without falling over. She grinned, proud of herself. "I'm not a flagon of mead. I don't break that easily. Do you think I'll be able to run in this castle you're taking me to, or is there a special dungeon prepared for me that's smaller than this one?" She'd never seen a castle, but envisioned it as a sort of stone version of her father's longhouse. Or his hall, maybe. She could run the length of the hall, at least.

Heber laughed. "Lady Portia, this is a castle. It's huge. There's a practice yard inside the walls, or so my cousin says."

His cousin had helped build it, so Heber should know.

"So there'll be space where I can practice

shooting outside?" she asked hopefully.

"You shall see when you get there, my lady. Are you finished with your letter yet?" Grieve said.

Portia laid down her quill. "I am." She sent up a silent prayer for Lina's safety, and rose. "Let us go."

She fastened her cloak and took up her bundle as though this were an ordinary day, or night, but she couldn't stop the thrill she felt inside. She should be more frightened, but she was giddy at the thought of freedom.

In the harsh light of day, she could worry about the Wolf again and what he would do to her and Isla. Tonight, she intended to relish her first ride in longer than she liked to remember.

Her horse, a beast she did not know, sensed her excitement and pranced about like the animal had been locked up for too long, too.

"My lady, we must make haste!" Grieve said.

She grinned. "Haste, you say?" She squeezed the mare between her thighs and whispered a command, letting the horse have her head. The mare flew.

Startled shouts came from behind her as her men urged their horses to match her speed.

Portia laughed merrily. "I have not forgotten how to ride, boys. Have you? Let's see who reaches the castle first!"

Loch Findlugan was too far for a true race, but she held her own until she felt her horse growing tired and allowed her to slow. Her men caught up, muttering curses they normally would not voice. At least not around her.

"My lady…" Grieve began.

Portia turned innocent eyes on Grieve. "You did say we needed haste."

"That I did, but that's not something I need to remind you any more, I think. I wanted to show you that." Grieve seized her bridle and pointed.

From this height, she could see clear to Portnahaven…and what lay between. A sea of campfires, showing the sheer size of the Wolf's army. Thousands of men, surely. More than she'd ever seen, anywhere. Who could stand against an army like that?

"We do not stand a chance, do we? They will take what they want, and no one will stop them." Tears formed and fell. Tears for Isla, the precious island they would conquer.

They were already lost.

"Of course we do. We are the Southern Islanders, my lady. They may burn our homes, our harvest, our whole damn island, but our people will survive and rebuild. You will survive to lead them. I swear it." The same darkness that hid her tears concealed Grieve's expression, but Portia didn't need to see it to know.

"I don't want you to die for me, Grieve. Not you, not any of you."

His teeth glinted in the moonlight as he grinned. "Then you'd best pray the Wolf is a reasonable man who is willing to negotiate. After a week against Mason's walls, maybe he will be." He moved ahead to order their party into what he called a more defensible formation, before returning to her side.

The joy of the night-time ride began to pall sooner than Portia expected, but she did not complain. Anything to be out of her loft prison.

The sky was lightening as they approached

the loch. Portia had not been here since she was a child, and she'd read and reread her mother's scroll on the history of this place so many times in captivity that she knew every word by heart. Here was the seat of the original lords of this land. Her ancestors, through her mother's line. Her mother's people had carved those standing stones, weeping sweat and tears as they dragged them into place to honour deities long dead.

Or perhaps not, for there was a holiness to this place that hung over it like fog. Maybe the old gods had made their last stand here, and were buried in the mounds that ringed the loch round. Here, she and her men would make their last stand, too, before she was forced to surrender Isla and likely her maidenhead.

But not yet. The Wolf would have to breach other walls first, and mighty walls they were, too. Her breath caught in her throat as she took in the enormity of what Mason had built. The castle covered Council Island, so the waters of the loch lapped at the walls. Not all the way around, but then it had not rained for days. The water level would soon rise, and hide the island again.

She began to believe that maybe, just maybe, there was some hope left.

Two boats waited to take them to their island home, and Portia surrendered her horse to a man she didn't know, who swore he'd take care of the mare before sending her home. She glanced at Grieve, who was doing the same with his horse. Time to trust his judgement, she decided, for she was too tired to think any more.

Her boat drifted under a stone arch topped by a spiky metal gate. It was open to allow her entrance now, but the heavy chains holding it in place spoke of how quickly it could be lowered to keep the world out.

Dermot helped her out, and Portia found she needed his assistance, for her legs ached after the unaccustomed ride.

"Guard her," Grieve said, directing the rest of his men to search the place.

Dermot and Cowal stood by her side, staring up at the high walls as avidly as Portia did.

"It's huge," Cowal breathed. "You'd need a

dragon to get into this place."

Dermot laughed. "Didn't you hear? That dragon in Kasmirus is dead. Some knight slew it, and won himself a bride."

"As long as the Wolf doesn't have it. No one's sure how he manages to burn whole villages when it's pouring with rain. A dragon might do that."

"Someone would notice a honking great dragon in the isles by now!" Dermot scoffed. "If the Albans didn't see such a beast, then he doesn't have one. Maybe this Wolf is beast enough on his own."

Dermot and Cowal debated about how to beat wolves and dragons while Portia fought to stay awake.

"It's empty."

Portia blinked her eyes open. Damn, she'd fallen asleep on her feet. "Mm?"

"It's empty," Grieve repeated. "No one here but us. Now the servants are here, I shall shut the gate and you'll be safe, Lady Portia."

"Can I sleep?" she mumbled.

He laughed. "Yes, my lady. The men are preparing a pallet for you in the tower room.

Tonight, I'll have a bed brought up, but now you may rest."

"Where's the tower?" she slurred, looking around.

"With your permission, my lady."

Portia had her legs swept out from under her as Grieve lifted her in his arms. If she'd had the strength, she'd have shouted at him to put her down. But she did not, so she settled back and told herself she'd tell him off in the morning.

Behind her, the gates clanged shut, and darkness descended.

"You must let me in! You must!"

Shouted words woke her, and Portia struggled to rise. How long had she slept? It looked near noon, but it was hard to tell with so many clouds in the sky.

Loud clanging as someone rang the gates like they were a bell. "Let me in, damn you!"

Portia stuck her head out of the tower window.

Mason sat in a boat outside the gates, whacking at them with his oar. He shook his fist at her. "Let me in or I shall take a stick to you, like your father should have, you ugly whore!"

"Insulting my lady will not let you in, you great blubbery fool," Grieve shouted back from the walls above the gate. "In fact, I am honour bound to keep you out, for you threatened her, and I must keep her safe. Go back to your homeland, for you're not welcome here, or anywhere else on the Southern Isles."

"But there's an army on the way! An army of Vikens! The only safe place is inside those walls!" Mason insisted.

"Then I thank you for building them, as they will protect my lady. 'Tis a fitting parting gift you give her, after trespassing on her hospitality so long. Get you gone before they get here, man. For if they catch you outside the gates, they will squash you like the cockroach you are."

"What about your laws of hospitality?" Mason demanded.

"'Tis not my roof you lived under, nor my lady's. You may ask her father for shelter if you wish, but I've seen you shit upon guest right for too long to be stupid enough to offer it to the likes of you. Perhaps you should not have sent Lord Angus to fight so far away. Maybe if you hurry, you may reach his house before the Wolf's army do. Maybe he'll give you shelter if you offer to build him a castle such as this."

"I hope he gives that ugly whore you serve to his men, so that they may rape the bitch to death. She deserves no better," Mason shouted as he rowed back to shore.

Portia wanted to shout back in kind, but the barb in his words had hit home. Perhaps the man was right, and that would be her fate. She would rather take a dagger to her own breast first.

She slid down the wall to sit on the cold flagstone floor. Would she end her days in this prison?

"My lady, I will not let that happen." Grieve stepped into the tower room and closed the door behind him. He moved to the window and pulled the shutters closed, too, filling the room with shadows. "There is a reason why I chose this room for you instead of the lord's chamber, though the other is warmer. We have taken the room below you as our barracks, so anyone attacking the castle must fight their way through us before they can reach you. And if they do, then you must escape." He slid his fingers down the window frame, and pulled a section away from the wall. A dark void beckoned – a space within the walls Portia would never have guessed existed. "You must climb down, then follow the passage to the hidden door. There is a boat down there, so that you may row ashore. If the castle walls are breached, we will give you the time you need to get away." His eyes met hers, saying the words that he did not.

"I won't let you die for me, Grieve. None of you," Portia said.

He smiled faintly. "Lady Portia, you are the second most powerful lady I know, and not even you have the power to prevent that. I stand by my oath."

"And what of Lady Rhona?" Portia demanded.

"If nothing else, Rhona will avenge me. She has a temper that matches yours, my lady." He bowed. "Now, get some sleep, while it is still quiet. Or you'll wish you had, for there will be an end to peace once that army arrives."

She had to laugh at that. It was either that or cry.

Crying could wait until she had to make use of that secret passage, she promised herself. For if she descended into the darkness, all would be lost.

Twenty Eight

That blocky stone structure rising out of Loch Findlugan where Council Island should be was an abomination. The gods of the old faith would have struck it down with lightning, thunder and whatever else they had in their arsenal. He wished the new ones would do it instead, but he didn't think saints dealt in lightning. Pity. He'd happily hail it as a miracle if they did.

At least his army were getting better at setting up camp, though he had to admit the failing light hurried them along better than he could. No one wanted to be caught out in the rain without their tent up. Not when they'd marched in it all day.

Perhaps they were too tired to start any fights tonight, was all. Or awed by the place where they stood – for Loch Findlugan was the home of Council Island, a holy place where no Islander was allowed make war on another.

And he'd brought war to it.

Lord Angus would never forgive him for this. 'Twas a good thing he wasn't here to see it.

Rudolf would not have done this if it was an Islander who held Portia prisoner. No, he'd have called the man out and the battle would have been between just the two of them, as was proper. But the Albans had brought in their army and fortified Council Island itself. He had no choice. Better that it was a Viken leading this army and not an Islander, then, even if Islanders outnumbered the Vikens in his army.

He'd been considering possible attack strategies since the castle came into view, and he still had nothing. How did one attack a rock? Not even Rhona could burn stone. In all his years of fighting, ambushing and being ambushed in Viken and on the Southern Isles, he'd never come up against something like this. You couldn't climb those smooth walls the way you scaled a cliff. And the damn thing was in the middle of a lake, with no sign of the boat fleet that had carried him to the island last time. A tiny coracle was the only craft he could see – a one-man craft that might take two or even three, if they were slight and didn't mind the closeness. Children, maybe, or two women…

He would not need to attack if he offered them something they wanted. More than anything, he wanted an end to this war. If Portia was safe, he would be willing to trade almost anything.

Portia was the politician, as astute as her father, or Lord Lewis. Rudolf was a warrior and a strategist. She would know what to offer, when all he wanted was her.

A trade, perhaps. If he offered the Albans her sisters as hostages, perhaps they'd be willing to negotiate. Maybe even open the gates...

Lina settled Arlie in the boat, shoving a cushion between her sister's back and the gunwale. "If anything happens to her or the babe because of you, Wolf, I and my kin will hunt you to the ends of the earth to exact our vengeance."

Rudolf nodded. Coward that he was, he couldn't look her in the eye, so he'd worn his helm for this. Full battle dress, in fact, as he paced along the shore, letting those in the castle get a good look at him.

A young Eriskan lad had volunteered to row the ladies across the lake. He looked no bigger than Rudolf himself had been the day he arrived at the Southern Isles, but he had the same courage. And so Rudolf had agreed, letting the most vulnerable members of his army assault the castle. For they had a better chance of gaining entry than he.

His men lined the shore, and theirs lined the battlements, watching the coracle's progress as it rippled between them. Could two armies hold their breath? For it seemed the only sound he could hear was the plash of oars as the two flame-haired girls retreated from him.

A third flash of orange at the tower's top window stopped his heart. Portia!

He wanted to fly across the water and take her in his arms, but she was as far out of reach as heaven itself right now. Even her face was out of view – hidden by her hair as she faced the oncoming boat, not him. She'd seen her sisters, all right.

She turned her head further still, meeting the eyes of…was it one of the men on the battlements? She gestured imperiously, her meaning clear. She wanted them to let her sisters in.

One of the armoured men on the battlements let out a shout, waving his arms with as much energy as Portia.

Was he commanding his men to open the gates, or fire on the defenceless boat? Surely no man of honour would open fire. They couldn't…

The gate at the waterline began to rise.

Lina shouted and pointed, and the Eriskan boy headed for the opening gate.

The boat slid into the darkness before the

gate clanged shut once more. His army began to disperse, heading for their tents or whatever they wanted to do while they waited. Polish their armour, perhaps.

But Rudolf was rooted to the shore, his eyes fixed on the tower window that no longer held the flaming beauty who'd haunted his dreams for so long.

Gods help him, from the old faith and the new. He'd sacrificed a boy, two women and an unborn babe just for the hope of seeing her again.

He hoped Portia would forgive him if he failed.

Twenty-Nine

Despite all her talk of wanting to run and shoot and do all the things she hadn't done in the barracks hall, Portia found herself peering out the window just like she had when she lived in the loft. She could sit in the tower windows, if she'd wanted to, but the stone was too cold, so she hung back, not wanting to touch it. There was plenty to see.

The army came in an orderly column, creeping into the valley like ants until they grew into men and settled on the shore where her own men had left their horses. The beasts were gone now, back to her father's stables with a groom, for there were no stables here to house them. Most of the army marched on foot, with a few hooded or armoured figures on horseback.

The Wolf Prince could be no one other than the proud peacock who led them, probably insisting no one else could ride before him lest they kick up dust or mud that might foul the highly polished sheen of his armour. His poor horse had to bear the weight of not just him, but all his weapons, too, for the man had sword, shield, axe, bow…he carried an armoury on his back, as though he expected an attack at any time. And so he should. A Viken who attacked the Southern Isles was an oathbreaker of the worst kind, breaking an alliance that had stood for centuries.

She wanted to take up her bow and shoot him then and there, but she knew he was out of range. Even from this height, she was too far from shore to shoot anything not on the lake's surface. If he could be persuaded to board a boat, though…

The tiny coracle Mason had left in the mud

wouldn't stand up to more than a few well-placed arrows before the holes in the hide let in enough water to sink it. Wearing so much armour, the Wolf was sure to sink, and good riddance.

His army set up camp with alarming efficiency, which surprised her when she realised only the first few ranks of troops were Viken. The lines marching over the hill now were unmistakeably Islanders – so many men! She hadn't known there were that many men on all the Southern Isles, yet here they were.

Why?

Why would her own people follow a man who burned their homes and killed their families? No man of the Isles would throw away his own honour in such a way. He'd kill the Wolf with his own hands, for sure.

For the first time, she began to doubt the tales she'd heard. That the Albans feared him, she'd known. But her own people…they weren't stupid. They wouldn't stand by and watch their own people die.

Did they believe the Wolf was their ally? Big and vulpine, perhaps, but not so bad?

The vast army made themselves at home on the valley floor, while the Wolf paced the camp. He was a big man, bigger than most, and he'd pitched his own tent in the centre of the camp, bigger than the rest, of course. The cloaked riders favoured the second largest tent, on the far edge of camp, away from the water. Three of them. One waddled like he was as fat as Mason, but there was something about the way the figure walked that made her certain it wasn't him. Besides, an Alban among this army would be in chains, or tied to a stake. Not free to walk about the camp.

"Have you never seen an army before?"

Portia looked up to meet Grieve's raised eyebrows. "Not like this one."

"Me, neither. Now I know what Lord Angus faces in Alba. 'Tis a fearsome sight." He held out the covered bowl he'd carried up the stairs. "I brought your dinner. Seeing as you didn't come to the dining hall with the rest of us…"

She took the bowl. "Thank you. I suppose I have spent so long alone, I am not accustomed to…to…"

"Freedom?" Grieve supplied. "This is all new to me, too, my lady. There is what I know, and then there is…this." He waved at the view.

"What are they doing?" Portia leaned out of the window, to get a better look. "They're sending someone out in the boat."

Two of the cloaked figures. Witches? Priests? She couldn't be sure. They were accompanied by an Islander boy who rowed the boat like he'd been born to it. A fisherman's son, probably. But the cloaked riders…

The Wolf stood on shore, speaking to the riders. Together, they reached up and lowered their hoods.

Portia let out a shriek. "It's Lina and Arlie! My sisters! And Arlie…Arlie's pregnant!" She pointed at the girl's belly. "I'm going to be an aunt!"

Grieve swore and bolted down the stairs.

"If you don't let them in, I'll open the gates myself!" she called after him.

Soon after, he appeared on the battlements, gesticulating wildly as he argued with Brian. More than once, he stabbed a finger in her direction. Finally, Brian headed down to the gates.

Portia watched the boat sail beneath the castle, before it was her turn to race down the stairs. She was breathless by the time she reached the bottom, but she didn't slow. It had been too long since she'd seen her sisters.

They clambered up the steps, looking just as tired as she'd been when she first arrived. Of course, they'd been riding all day.

Portia issued orders for a feast to be prepared, and for water to be brought up to her room so that they might wash, for where else would they sleep? The enormous bed was more than big enough for three of them.

She wasn't sure who to hug first. Arlie, lest her baby decide to arrive this very moment, or Lina, who she'd only just missed?

Grieve stood beside them with a grave look on his face. "Tell them what you told me."

Arlie's face crumpled as she burst into tears, leaving Lina to say the words: "We are here as the Wolf's envoys. He offers everyone in the castle safe passage off Isla, if they open the gates and lay down their weapons."

Portia's mouth was dry. It was too easy. It must be a trick of some kind. Or..."What does the Wolf ask in return?"

"That King Donald gives up all claim to the Southern Isles and its people..."

Portia had expected that, and she would happily support it.

"...and that you surrender Portia to the Wolf."

Even Lina leaked a few tears as she said it, though she quickly wiped them away. "I'm sorry, Portia. That's what he wants."

"What does he want of me?" she asked.

"It doesn't matter. He shall not have her!" Grieve said.

The men on the walls rumbled their agreement.

"How long do I have?" Portia whispered.

"It does not matter. He will have to tear down the walls and kill every man among us before he can touch you!"

"He wants your answer by noon tomorrow," Lina said.

Portia nodded. She blinked back tears. Tomorrow, it would be time to end this.

"Then tonight we shall have a feast, to remind us of happier times, and tomorrow, he will have his answer," Portia said.

"His answer lies at the point of my sword!"

Portia linked arms with Arlie and Lina. "Come, I'll take you to my chamber where we may wash while the men make plans for the morrow."

It took some time to help Arlie up the stairs, and even longer to catch her breath. Being cooped up in that loft had not done her any good. She hoped the Wolf would let her see the sun a little, at least. What there was of it.

While Arlie collapsed on the bed, complaining about how her back hurt, Lina pulled Portia aside. "There's something else. I didn't want to say it in front of all those angry men out there, for they are beyond reason right now."

"What is it?"

"It's Rudolf."

Portia's mouth was dry once more, and she feared it might be a desert until the day she died now. "What news of Rudolf?"

Lina wet her lips. "He's down there. He

rides with them, Portia. This is the help he brought, at our father's command. Most of the men are our people, fighting to be free of the Albans. They fight with the Wolf, not against him."

"And Rudolf?"

"He has the Wolf's favour, I am certain of it. Because he was the one who took us prisoner, and it was nothing like I had heard. He has treated us as well as any of the men in that vast horde. Food, a place to sleep, a tent to keep the rain off…horses to ride, while the men march. None of the Vikens has laid a finger on us, and no man among them has even hinted at it. They fear the Wolf's wrath." Lina gripped her shoulder. "Portia, make your men see sense. When they surrender, you'll get to see Rudolf again. Isn't that worth it?"

She wanted to say that it was. A week ago, she might have given anything to see Rudolf again. But to see the man she'd loved for as long as she could remember as she surrendered herself to another man? A man who owned his allegiance, as he would own her, too?

Darkness lay on her heart, as never before.

This morning, she thought she could bear whatever the Wolf would do to her. But if Rudolf had to watch? It would break her heart.

She forced a smile for her sisters. "No more talk of war, or the morrow. Tonight we feast, and talk of the past. For I have missed much, it seems. I know Arlie was always a greedy guts, but when did she learn to eat melons whole?"

The talk turned to lighter things, but the darkness within remained. Later, she would surrender to it. Now…she had her last supper to enjoy.

Thirty

Portia waited until her sisters had fallen asleep before she crept over to the window. Despite their protestations about receiving kind treatment from the Wolf, their journey from their burned homes to here could not have been an easy one. They would sleep for some hours yet – so soundly, perhaps, that they wouldn't notice her absence at all.

Night air puffed through the window, chilling her bare arms. It was colder out here on the loch and the stone walls seemed to drink the chill, making the castle colder still.

Portia dressed quickly, trusting her long skirt and cloak to protect her from the biting breeze. Stockings and shoes would only slow her down tonight.

Her bow and quiver might come in useful, though. She slipped her finger into the quiver, questing until she found what she sought. She stashed the pouch in the pocket of her cloak before slinging the bow and quiver over her shoulder, leaving her hands free.

Placing both hands on the wintry stone, she climbed onto the windowsill. It was wide enough for her and her sisters to have used it for a bed, or for her to stand there while she opened the hinged section of the timber window frame to reveal the secret passage.

A whiff of the fish oil that she'd used to silence the hinges reached her nostrils, but it was better than a loud squeak rousing sound sleepers. She would endure far more discomfort before this evening was through.

A ladder led down into the darkness between the castle's inner and outer walls. A passage to freedom or, in this case, answers.

Portia twisted, trying to step from the sill to

the ladder, but something caught on the window frame, holding her back. Cursing quietly, she backed up. It was the bloody bow, of all things. Which wouldn't be much use if she ran into trouble – she was better at shooting enemies from a distance. Stabbing someone with an arrow was silly, especially when she already had a dagger. Portia considered for another moment, then unhooked the offending thing from her shoulder and dropped it on the floor. The quiver clattered down atop it, and Portia winced, wishing she hadn't been so loud.

Her gaze darted to the bed, where her sisters slept on.

She allowed herself to breathe again.

The ladder rungs were rough under her feet, making her wish she'd brought her boots, but she refused to return for them now. Instead, she pulled the window panel closed to hide her descent.

Darkness cloaked her, settling like a layer of wet wool. Or was that her dread at what waited for her? Not in the darkness, but across the loch.

If dread weighed her down, at least it gave her the push she needed to keep climbing down until her feet sank into sucking mud. Trying not to think of corpses sucking at her toes each time she took a step, corpses of the men who would die tomorrow if she failed, Portia made her way along the secret passage to its hidden entrance, or exit, in her case.

She stumbled over the boat Grieve had told her would be there, but she didn't take it. Not yet. She'd memorised her mother's scroll, and if it was correct, there was another, more ancient way across the loch that didn't require rowing.

She continued down the passage until she found what she sought.

A timber half door, covered in a thin layer of stone to conceal its true nature from the outside world, yielded to her touch. Its hinges were not so silent, but there was no one about to hear their squeaky protest.

Moonlight turned the loch into a mirror, for there was no breeze down here. No need, for the air was positively frigid. Portia scanned the shore, looking for the standing stones she knew had to be there. Stones that had seen the passage of so many people, yet they would still stand after this battle, sentinels of time.

One...and then she found the second, a finger pointing at the sky as if to remind her that she could only hide in darkness, so she only had until dawn to find her answers.

She edged around the castle walls, knowing she had to line the stones up properly to be certain she stood in the right place. Her ancestors had done this from time immemorial, or so her mother's history scroll had said. There was no need to be frightened of following in their footsteps.

But her ancestors had not faced a legend, a man who'd had so many stories spun about him that he seemed the very devil himself. And yet...her sisters' safety spoke of someone who understood chivalry and honour, who might save what others sought to destroy.

She wasn't sure what to believe any more. She dreaded, and yet she hoped.

Which was why she would face him alone.

Portia paused to squint at the stones again. Now she could only see one – perfectly aligned. She took a deep breath, and stepped into the loch.

Icy water swirled around her feet, and her breath huffed out in a startled cloud of condensation. Her boots would not save her from the loch, but she wished she'd worn them anyway, if only for an extra moment's warmth before they grew sodden and slowed her down.

She held her hem high to keep it from getting wet, until she realised that the water didn't even reach her ankles. She let the fabric fall, lifting her gaze to the stones to keep her on her course. The ancient causeway lay hidden beneath the surface of the loch and one wrong step would result in a ducking. Her nearly numb feet already found it hard to feel the stones, so she must maintain her vigilance.

The shore came closer and closer, and Portia dared to hope she might reach it before the numbness spread to her knees.

She was only a few yards away when a male voice demanded, "Halt!"

She blew out a breath she hadn't known she'd been holding.

Hope sank to the bottom of the loch, threatening to drown her courage with it.

Thirty-One

"I told you ghosts don't take orders!" one voice insisted.

"They might. She might have been a really obedient wife in life. How many spirits have you seen?" a second voice reasoned.

"It doesn't matter. She's walking on water. That makes her a ghost, or a witch."

"It's angels that walk on water, you fool! The devil's servants sink!"

"I heard a sailor at Beacon Isle tell the story of a woman who walked on water. She was a witch. She could see into men's souls to decide whether to sink your ship or save you, they said."

"There are good men and bad in every bunch, or on every ship. How'd she know which ships to sink if there were both kinds of men aboard?"

"I don't know – do I look like a witch?"

"You look like the idiot who just ordered a ghost to halt."

"Well, she did, didn't she? She even gave you a gift."

Rudolf listened to the exchange with amusement, but his curiosity got the better of him. This was his army camp, and no one got in or out without his knowledge. Not even a ghost.

"The gift's not for me. It's for the commander, she said. If she is a witch, maybe she's trying to curse him."

Rudolf poked his head out of his tent. "What is this cursed gift?"

The two men stopped, looking sideways at each other until one of them said, "It's like this, sir. There's a lady out on the lake who walks on water, who asked me to give you this." He set the small pouch on Rudolf's outstretched palm.

He weighed it for a moment, wondering if it was empty.

"I have heard of a woman who can walk on water. A witch so powerful that water obeys her. She used to live at Beacon Isle, but now she wears a crown. Queen Margareta, her name is, and her kingdom is not too far north of here," Rudolf said.

"Begging your pardon, sir, but what would a queen be doing out on yon lake so late at night?" the gift-bearer asked.

Rudolf emptied the pouch into his hand. "Handing out gifts, or so it would seem."

Both men recoiled and crossed themselves. "Dead virgins' fingers! That must be a powerful curse, sir. Throw them away before the magic takes hold!"

Rudolf prodded one of the pale fingers. It was hollow, as were its companions. When he turned them over, he found the lacings holding them together. The finger guards were so well-worn they still held the shape of their mistress's fingers. Portia would not abandon these on the eve of battle.

Unless she intended to stop the battle from taking place.

Rudolf tucked the finger guards safely back in their pouch. "Take me to this woman. I must see her for myself."

The two men hesitated, before the one who hadn't spoken yet ventured, "Sir, is that you issuing orders, or are you under the influence of the witch's curse?"

"Make me ask again, and you'll be on latrine duty until next year. Both of you," Rudolf stressed.

"Yes, sir!"

They trotted off, hunting hounds eagerly leading the way to his quarry.

Or so Rudolf hoped. If the lady had gone...

Yet as he reached the lake's edge, his breath caught in his throat. There was someone standing in the water, though she appeared to be floating on its surface. Now he understood why his men had mistaken her for a ghost.

Rudolf extended his hand. "Why don't you come ashore, my lady?" he asked.

She turned so that the hood's shadow hiding

her face pointed toward him. "Would you step ashore, knowing the land is occupied by an enemy's army?"

Rudolf pulled the finger guards from their pouch. "The lady who owns these will never be my enemy. I promised to protect her, and my promise still stands."

She lifted her hands to her hood, ready to lower it. "What can you tell me of the man they call the Wolf Prince?"

"A highborn Viken, cousin to the king, commander of this army and conqueror of the Southern Isles." It sounded quite impressive, laid out like that. Maybe it would impress her enough to make her forget how long he'd been away.

"Not this isle. Not yet," she said fiercely.

No, it was not enough to impress Portia.

Rudolf spread his arms wide. "Look again, Lady. This army has already taken Isla. The only holdout is that tiny fort on the lake, and it will not hold out for much longer."

"A week," she said softly, as though it pained her.

"You think it will take that long?" He

wanted to say that he could take it in a day, if she needed him to do so. For if this was truly Portia, he would scale the walls alone to save her. Yet here she stood, hardly a prisoner.

"We only have enough food for a week. I know the state of the castle store rooms, and how much we eat. Lina would not have made the same mistake, but I was not prepared for a siege with so many mouths to feed. I do not wish my people to die. I want to sue for peace."

"Name your terms."

Her head darted to the left and right. "First, take me to the Wolf's tent, where we might discuss this in private. Can you give me that?"

"Of course."

She nodded. "Do you swear to grant me safe passage into your camp?"

Into it, but not out. Interesting. "I do so solemnly swear."

"Then take me there, Dolf."

He held his hand out once more, more out of courtesy than any expectation that Portia would need it, until she stumbled. Courtesy be damned. He dived forward to catch her.

"Release me." It was a command.

He set her on her feet on the grass before he did as she asked.

She tugged her hood down. "Lead the way, Dolf."

It took all his willpower not to glance back over his shoulder as he took her to his tent. Now, he wished he'd accepted the hospitality of one of the nearby crofters so that he could offer her something better than this. Portia deserved better than this.

He straightened the coverlet on his pallet, as though he hadn't been roused from sleep by her arrival. The ancient laws of hospitality demanded that he offer her something to eat and drink, but he had nothing here. His tent was a place to sleep. Nothing more.

Rudolf stepped out of his tent and hailed the first man he saw. "Bring me a jug of mead," he said.

The jug was brought. Too late, Rudolf realised he should have asked for cups to go with it.

He re-entered his tent, and there she stood.

Her red hair glowed in the firelight of his

brazier, haloing her like the saint who had given Loch Findlugan its name.

"Portia," he breathed. It came out like a prayer to heaven. A prayer that after all he'd endured, this angel might become his.

"Dolf?" she asked uncertainly. "I have watched the Wolf striding around the camp in that armour all day. This is his tent. Tell me the truth now, for I must know. Who is he?"

Thirty-Two

Rudolf set the jug on the ground and bowed. "Prince Rudolf Vargssen, cousin to Reidar Haraldssen, King of Viken. Reidar's father and mine were brothers."

Oh, how she didn't want to believe it. But how could she not believe him? "So you are the Wolf. The man who has killed, raped and plundered his way across the Southern Isles to take my home from me."

Rudolf shook his head. "I swear to you, I am the Wolf, but I have done none of those things. I have never raped a woman, nor killed one since I set foot on the Southern Isles. Not even my aunt, who would not have been so kind to me. I have killed men, it is true, though they tried equally hard to kill me. As for plunder..." He waved at the unadorned interior of his tent. "Do you see anything of worth here? I have taken nothing from the islands that was not given to me freely. The lords of the isles are with me. All but your father, who I'd hoped to find here with you. As for your home..." He ducked his head. "I may have set fire to it. Just a little," he admitted.

"But Mason and his men said..."

"Is Mason your husband?" Rudolf demanded.

Portia had never seen such pain in his eyes. "Mason is Donald's man, sent here to secure the islands for Alba. And build high walls to keep people both out and in." Her gaze arrowed in the direction of the castle on Council Island.

"Is he your husband?"

Portia laughed bitterly. "Mason who thinks so much of himself? No. He believes I am beneath his notice. The fat pig of a man desires one of Donald's daughters, and he thinks subduing us will earn him that honour. He holds me safe from Viken raiders and other unscrupulous men, who might want to marry me for their own ends. More likely, he thinks to marry me off to whoever Donald sends to replace him. One of Donald's sons, he said."

"If you are a prisoner, how did you get out?"

She shook her head. "I cannot tell you that. The Dolf I once knew would not ask me to betray my sisters by letting the leader of an enemy army into the chamber where they sleep."

If anything, her words had hurt him even more.

"I have never been, and will never be your enemy, Portia."

For a long moment, she stared at him. Heaven help her, but she believed him.

All the fear and frustration and years of missing him and dreading the future bubbled up. She swallowed back a sob. She couldn't cry now. She had a peace agreement to broker with the Wolf, who was not the Dolf she'd known before the war. This man was harder, commanding armies and conquering islands. Conquering her island.

"What terms will you offer us, then, so that my people and yours are not enemies?" Portia said. Oh, but it hurt to call the other Islanders his people. This man was a foreigner to her, while she'd considered them friends. Once considered him a friend.

Rudolf shook his head. "That's not how it works. I have given the castellan my terms. I will let everyone in the castle go, unharmed, if they lay down their arms and release you."

"He cannot. Grieve swore an oath to my father, he and all his men, that they would protect me."

"But he does not have you now. I do. What will he do if you do not return?" Triumph glittered in Rudolf's eyes, something else she'd never seen there before.

Something died inside Portia. "Then Grieve and his men will come in search of me, even if it means attacking the camp. We both know they would die. Grieve is a good man, and so are those who serve under him. Good men, loyal to my father, and loyal to me. They don't deserve to die. Not yet."

"And what do I deserve? I have fought for years for this. For these islands. For your home."

She closed her eyes to stop the tears from falling. She should have sent Lina to negotiate on her behalf. Lina's knees would not have weakened at the longing in Rudolf's tone.

"You can have the islands. All of them. And my home. As long as you promise to spare them, too."

Rudolf shook his head. "They must lay down their arms, yet you say they will not. I once vowed to protect you, too, and I would fight as long as I had the breath left to shout a battle cry. If these men are as loyal as you say, they will fight to the death – theirs or ours."

"Or mine." It came out as a whisper, but Portia couldn't stop it.

"Never," Rudolf swore. He seized her shoulders. "There must be another way, Portia. I let go of you once, and I will not lose you now. Not to Donald or Mason or any man who dares to lay claim to you and your birthright." He dropped to his knees. "I will give you everything I've fought for. Every island, every rock, every fishing boat. For you."

Her breath caught in her throat. He couldn't mean...

"What would you ask in return?" she asked faintly, pressing her hand to her breast to hide her hammering heart.

"You. Other men may desire your dowry, but all I've ever wanted is you." He held out his hands in supplication. "Marry me, Portia."

All her adult life she'd wanted to hear those words, dreading the day she'd have to refuse him. Tonight, she'd come to offer herself to the Wolf, knowing it would cut her off from Rudolf forever. But now...

"If Grieve came in search of me, he could not break a marriage bond," Portia said thoughtfully. "My claim would pass to you, my husband. If I stand at your side as your wife, Grieve would open the castle gates to you."

She'd said something wrong. The shining love in Rudolf's eyes had gone. Had she imagined it?

Rudolf rose. "Of course. You think of your men. This Grieve must mean much to you." He sounded bitter.

"Until my father returns home, they are the last of his men. Just as they swore to protect me, I have a responsibility to them," Portia said. She had little choice, and it lightened her heart enough to see her way clearly for the first time. "Yes." Her father would understand. Rudolf had been her heart's choice, long ago, when she could not have him. As the Wolf Prince, she could. Hope blossomed. "But it must be tonight, before anyone notices I am gone. Or someone will die."

He eyed her. "A marriage is not valid without vows to be faithful, followed by a consummation. We must do that tonight, too."

She swallowed. Consummating a marriage was the hardest part. She'd never forget Lina's or Arlie's cries of pain on their wedding nights. Dolf might protect her, but he could not save her from himself. It was but a small price to pay to end a war. "It shall be as you say. We must wake the priest who serves Saint Findlugan's church, and ask him to marry us."

Thirty-Three

"I wish you both well. You may...you may use my house for the consummation. I shall return in the morning," Father Fintan said, ducking out the door and into the rain before Rudolf could stop him.

Rudolf and Portia stared at each other for a moment. His heart sank at the fear in her expression. He'd dreamed of this night for half his life, but never had he imagined his first night with her would be in a tiny, cold cottage with a straw pallet so thin and narrow they may as well be making love on the floor like animals. He'd imagined a roaring fire, a room so warm she'd want to take her clothes off, and a big, carved bed like the one he'd slept in in Viken.

"We don't have to do this if you do not wish to," Rudolf said.

She tossed her head. "We do. My father, Mason and this bloody king of his will dissolve a marriage that hasn't been consummated as quickly as salt in a stew pot." She hoisted her skirts up to her waist. "Where would you have me, husband?"

Husband. The word sounded so good on her lips, and yet…there was no love in the way she said it. Like his firebrand of a wife had died inside by marrying him.

Rudolf dismissed the priest's pallet, but that left him little more to choose from. He wanted to hold her close, to kiss her, to make her comfortable when he made love to her for the first time.

Reidar had made his bride scream for joy on their wedding night. They'd known each other for barely two days, and the whole castle had known just how much the queen loved her king. Rudolf had loved Portia for half his life, and he vowed he would show her that tonight.

Women enjoyed lovemaking more when they were on top, he'd heard, so Portia must mount him. That mean..."There," he said, pointing at a bench by the wall. He sat down on the broad seat, and patted his knees. "Sit here, my lady."

With some difficulty, owing to her bundled up skirts, Portia climbed into his lap. Gently, Rudolf guided her around to face him, so she straddled him.

"This is not how my sisters did it," she protested. "Their husbands made them lie down and..." She paled and didn't finish.

"When we have a bed worthy of you, I shall lay you down upon it, and show you every pleasure a man can give a woman," Rudolf promised. "But tonight, it is here or the floor, I'm afraid."

He could feel the heat of her, now, burning through his tunic. With her skirts so high, she was naked to the waist, and he longed to stroke her lovely legs right until he reached the apex where they met and then...

She squirmed in his lap. "Why are you so hard?"

His cock only hardened further in response. He freed it from the folds of his clothes and laid it beside her leg. "Because you are so beautiful," he said.

She didn't seem to hear him. Her alarmed gaze was fixed on his cock. "You're going to stick that huge thing into me?"

He wanted to laugh, but he feared that wouldn't help. He'd never seen his fearless Portia look so frightened. "Actually, the way we're sitting, you'll be in control of that. I'll just position it right, and all you have to do is sink down on it, as slowly as you like."

"Very well."

She rose. If she hadn't been wearing her clothes, Rudolf could have kissed her breasts. Next time they made love, he vowed, they'd be naked and he'd kiss them for twice as long to make up for it. Maybe even suck on her nipples a bit, too, if she liked that.

His cock was rock hard now, jutting toward her so eagerly it took all his willpower not to grab her hips and slam her down upon it. They had all night, he reminded himself. All night to take this as slowly as she needed.

Portia set her hands on his shoulders and glanced down. "It looks even bigger now. Are you sure it will fit?"

"Of course," he soothed, cupping one hand around her bottom to bring her closer. He wrapped his other hand around his shaft, positioning the head of his cock right against her sweet spot. One small push and the irresistible heat of her engulfed the tip. He sucked in a breath, fighting down the urge to thrust hard and deep into her. "Now, just sink down and I'll slide right in."

He closed his eyes, savouring the feel of her. Her nails dug into his shoulders as her molten heat embraced him, inch by inch, so tight he wanted to moan in bliss. He had to let her control this. He had to. Because if he did…in two or three thrusts he'd be done, she felt so incredibly good.

He cupped her bottom in both hands now, squeezing her soft flesh to stop himself from pushing her all the way down in one mighty shove.

And then, in one delicious eternity, she'd sheathed him completely, clenched down so hard on him that Rudolf feared his cock would blow then and there. He didn't dare move, she felt so exquisite. "God, Portia, that feels amazing."

She let out a sound that sounded like a sob.

Rudolf's eyes flew open.

Tears streamed down Portia's cheeks. "Please, finish this quickly, Dolf. It hurts so!"

He shifted and she cried out – definitely not in pleasure.

"Please," she begged.

He ripped his cock out of her as if he'd burned it, as well he might have. He tucked himself away, swearing at himself for being such a fool. Portia stumbled back, away from him, clutching her skirts to her face as she sobbed into them.

A thin trickle of blood ran down her thigh. Maiden's blood, for Portia was a maiden no more. He'd seen to that, and pretty damn clumsily, too.

Rudolf rose and sat Portia down on his seat. He found a bucket of water and a cloth, cleaning off the blood before she could see it. She cried out as he touched the cloth to her lower lips and Rudolf stopped. He'd dealt with most of the mess.

He dropped the cloth in the bucket and smoothed down Portia's skirts before he took her in his arms. "Shh, it's all right. It's over, it's over. Everything's put away, so you just hold onto me and cry as much as you need to."

God, she felt good in his arms, too. Not quite as good as she did with his cock buried balls deep in her, but nearly. Nearly. Maybe another night, when –

"Please don't make me do that again, Dolf. It hurt so much!" Portia begged.

Maybe never. Rudolf sighed. Who'd have thought he'd have such a clumsy cock? So much for giving his bride a blissful wedding night, or any night, for that matter.

"I'll never do anything to hurt you, Portia. I swear it." He swallowed. "And there's no need for more. The marriage is consummated. You did it. You and everyone on your island are safe. No one can dissolve our marriage now."

He held her as she cried herself out,

murmuring endearments aloud even as he silently cursed himself. He had what he wanted – the wife of his dreams, and all the Southern Isles. So why did victory feel as cold and miserable as stroking his own cock in the rain?

Because that's what he'd be doing, as soon as Portia fell asleep, he told himself, so he wouldn't frighten her with the sight of him again. But in the meantime, he could hold her close and love her, in whatever way she wanted. Because one thing was certain – Rudolf loved his wife, and he'd do anything for her.

Thirty-Four

Portia awoke cold and stiff, like she'd slept on the stone. And with ache between her legs that reminded her…

Rudolf. He'd returned, and she'd married him last night. She'd known he was too big, but she'd done it anyway. And now he was…

Not here.

But it couldn't have been a dream!

She wouldn't have dreamed such a terrible wedding night. Not with Rudolf. Heaven help her, she'd cried herself to sleep in his arms.

No wonder he was gone.

"Good morning, my lady. Do you wish to break your fast?"

Portia sat up. The middle aged priest who'd married them last night stood by the table with his head bowed, as if not daring to look at her.

"Or perhaps you would like to wash?"

Memories of Rudolf's hands on her thighs as he cleaned the most intimate parts of her made her blush. What must he think of her?

She turned suspicious eyes on the priest. "Do you know who I am?"

He smiled. "Of course, Lady Portia. Prince Rudolf was most adamant that I take good care of you until he returns to collect you. He even sent a man with breakfast, so that you might not go hungry. This is more than a poor priest usually sees unless he is invited to a feast." He waved at the table. "I look forward to the feast when they make him High Lord of the Isles, as is his due."

"What?" Her father was High Lord of the Isles, not Rudolf. Rudolf didn't hold lands here. He was a Viken prince. He probably owned an ice floe somewhere in Viken.

"I remember the first council meeting Lord

Angus brought him to. He was the first man ashore, at Lord Angus's behest. I knew it then, but it is even more clear now. Prince Rudolf will rule us well."

Rule? Rudolf? She'd married him, but…

The priest coughed. "Sorry, my lady. I forget that you are a new bride and perhaps have other things on your mind. Many new brides see their husband differently in the light of day after their wedding night. I often have to remind them that if they lay with their husband often enough, he will never stray, and may soon bless her with strong sons or beautiful daughters. I counsel – "

"Where is Rudolf now?" Portia interrupted. She had no need for a lecture on her marital duties from a man who knew little about them.

"I imagine he is with his army, preparing for battle."

"No!"

"I am sure he will return when it is all over. He asked that I keep you safe."

"To blazes with safe. There should be no battle. Good men will die if he continues with this stupidity." She smoothed her dress, retying her laces though she did not need to. "Do you possess a comb?" Heaven help her, but she would not turn up at an army camp with straw in her hair.

"Of course, my lady. No mirror, though, but sometimes I find the collection plate is shiny enough to see myself." He held up the bronze dish, and Portia peered at her reflection.

She cursed as she saw the straw in her hair. Combing the mess would be more painful than coupling with Rudolf last night, but she must. She made short work of it, then thanked the priest for his help.

"Eat, my lady." The priest pushed the bread toward her.

She did not have time, yet she must. Portia seized a piece of bread in one hand and a chunk of cheese in the other. She could eat on the way.

The priest helped her fasten her cloak, and she burst outside into the late morning sun. Nearly noon. She broke into a run.

Thirty-Five

Just before noon, the gate opened to let out a boat bigger than the coracle Rudolf had sent across the loch yesterday. With three armoured men aboard, it was no surprise. Two red heads watched from the tower window, but he knew neither belonged to Portia. No, she was safe with Father Fintan.

He'd ordered his men back from the lake shore, but they still stood to watch. Few wore weapons or armour as he did – this was supposed to be a peace negotiation. Yet the men in the boat looked ready for war.

As the three stepped ashore, one emerged as a definite leader. The castellan who'd ordered the gates open yesterday, Rudolf guessed. Was this Portia's man, Grieve, or someone else?

Rudolf removed his helm so that he might see them better. The men waited until they reached him before they did the same.

"Wolf," the castellan said, with the slightest nod. No, Rudolf did not know this man.

"Rudolf?" one of his companions said, nudging the third man. "We thought you'd buggered off back to Viken!"

"Damhan, Dermot," Rudolf greeted them after a moment's thought. "As you can see, I have returned."

Dermot grinned. "You never were one to run from a fight. I remember the day you arrived, I knocked you down once, but none of the other boys could touch you. You just got up and brushed it off. That's the day you found the Three Little Pigs!" His glee faded as quickly as it had come. "It seems we need your help again."

The castellan hushed him with a glare. "We are not here to ask for help. We are here to negotiate better terms than the ones you offered yesterday." He planted his feet firmly. "We will not hand over Lady Portia."

Won't, or can't? Rudolf wondered. Did they know she was missing?

"Did you ask Lady Portia?" he asked.

The three exchanged glances. Yes, they did, and yet they'd come to negotiate with him, knowing they had nothing he wanted. That took courage.

"What the lady wants is of no consequence. We have sworn an oath to protect her, and we will."

Rudolf snorted. He couldn't help it. "Have you even met Portia?"

This could not be Grieve. No man she spoke of so highly would try to peddle such nonsense.

He toyed with the idea of telling the man he was her husband. Then he'd have his answer, for no man who loved her could hide his pain at hearing that.

The castellan drew his sword. "Have you?"

A collective gasp rose from the men behind him. This was no way to conduct a peace negotiation.

"Sheath that thing, you bloody fool!"

The castellan's eyes widened and he nearly dropped his sword. "Rhona?"

"You lay one finger on this man, Wolf Prince, and our alliance is over!" Rhona said, striding to the man's side.

It seemed the alliance was over already.

Rudolf narrowed his eyes. "Who are you?"

The castellan opened his mouth, but it was Rhona who answered, "He's Grieve Lewisson, my betrothed, and the head of Lady Portia's personal guard." She turned on the man. "Why have the Albans sent you to negotiate?"

Damhan and Dermot burst out laughing. "What Albans? They've all fled, like the cowards they are. Even Mason, when we shut him out. Council Island and the castle belong to Lady Portia."

"No. It belongs to my husband." Portia's voice rang out over the water as she strode along the shore. She wore no shoes and her gown was muddied to the knees, but she walked like a queen. No sign of last night's downpour of tears. Now, she was the storm.

"Lady Portia! Thank the heavens!" Only now did Grieve sheathe his sword. "What happened to you? We thought...my lady, your boots!"

If his men hadn't noticed before, they did now.

But that's what he loved about Portia. Thousands of armed men watching, holding their collective breath, and she merely tossed her head and said, "I'm sure my husband will buy me new ones when he is done here." She laid a possessive hand on his arm, lining up beside him against Rhona and Grieve. She lifted her burning gaze to Rhona, something even Rudolf would have hesitated to do.

Should he warn her? he wondered, but there was no time.

"Lady Rhona," Portia said, offering the woman her cheek. "It is a pleasure. I have heard so much about you."

The two women kissed. A little stiffly, to be sure, for they were strangers, but the power play between them was palpable. The witch who terrified his men capitulated to Portia.

"I look forward to your wedding. You must

sit beside me at the feast to celebrate mine," Portia said. She shot a pointed look at Rudolf. "Of course, you and Grieve must sit with us at the high table. I insist."

"My lady," Grieve said weakly, looking from one woman to the other.

"I hope you mean Rhona, for I'm not yours any more. Protecting me is Prince Rudolf's job now." Her fingers squeezed his arm. "Isla is ours!"

Rudolf's men took up the cry until it echoed around the valley. He wanted to weep, but knew he could not.

The war was over, and Portia was safe. His to protect.

"But what will your father say?" Grieve asked.

Portia didn't flinch. "We will find out when he returns home. In the meantime, my husband will take his place in council."

And not a man among them dared argue. The Lady of Isla had spoken.

Thirty-Six

She smiled through her wedding feast and said all that needed to be said, but inside Portia felt empty. Rudolf would scarcely look at her, and every time she tried to get his attention, she'd find some lord or other already occupying it. He never even noticed when she bade him good night and headed up to her tower room, where she slept alone.

Her days were as dull as when she'd lived in the loft, for she saw so little of him, it was like she had no husband at all. At night, he did not come to her room, or summon her to his, as was his right. Why, she did not even know where he slept, or if he did. The lords never left him alone, and rumours circled, each wilder than the last.

Her men were hers no longer – they'd been pressed into doing things for their lordly fathers. Grieve had been sent to fetch Lord Lewis from Myroy, and there was talk of her father returning. Talk was all it was, until she saw the party riding over the ridge.

The men on lookout saw him, too. "Lord Angus! The banners of Isla!"

Preparations were made to turn the great hall into a council chamber, for there were important matters to be decided. Matters that could only be discussed here on Council Island.

Matters that she had no business being part of. So Portia sat alone in her tower, hoping her father might visit her when the meeting was over.

"There you are!" Lord Angus had other ideas, evidently. He'd aged, and he was now missing part of his ear. "Why are you not at Rudolf's side, in the thick of things, like you used to be?"

Portia managed a small smile. "Every time I see him, he has a lord on each arm, and a line of more men waiting to speak to him. He has no time for me. And there is talk of crowning him as King of the Southern Isles, an office we have never had. They wanted to do it right away, but Lord Lewis insisted we had to wait. For you, he said."

Angus nodded. "Aye, I've heard. It's been a long time coming, but it's for the best. Lord Lewis knew I would not want to miss the coronation of our first king."

"But you're the High Lord of the Isles! I thought he was your friend – why would he want you to answer such an insult in person?"

Angus laughed. "'Tis not an insult. He is a better man than me, and younger, too. I put him forward years ago, before Donald's army came to Isla. Rudolf will make a good king. Do you not think so?" He peered at her. "You chose the man, so surely you must."

"He will make an excellent king," Portia said warmly. She'd seen enough over the last few days to know that, if she did not already.

"But?"

She swallowed. "I thought he had feelings for me, instead of marrying me for my claim, like the others might have. But…"

Angus laughed so hard he nearly fell off the windowsill. "No feelings for you? Rudolf? That man's been in love with you since the day you donned a woman's gown. And I've seen the way you look at him, too. Why else do you think you got a personal guard while he was gone? It was not that he has the strength of ten men, though he is a mighty warrior. Nay, it was because I promised to keep you safe for him until he returned. He would never have left for Viken otherwise."

Portia couldn't seem to close my mouth. "But he has been so distant since we married. He hasn't…" She felt a blush burn her cheeks. "He hasn't summoned me to his chambers at all since our wedding night."

"Ah, he knows you too well, is all. Rudolf knows you are not the sort of woman he can order about. You'd punch him in the nose, or some more tender place, I'd wager, and he knows it. 'Tis up to you to come to him, I'm sure." It was his turn to blush. "Your mother came to me before we were married, and would not take no for an answer. She'd taken some fertility potion a witch had given her, and she wouldn't give herself to any man but me. I think we made you girls that night." He continued, too lost in reflection to realise that Portia had stopped listening.

Rudolf wanted her. Maybe even loved her. If her father could see it…

"Tonight," she said, so softly she didn't think her father heard. "Tonight, I shall bed the king.

Thirty-Seven

Rudolf stepped into the lord's chambers and slammed the door shut. Why in heaven's name had he agreed to be their king?

"Congratulations, my king." Portia stepped out of the shadows. The laces across her breasts had come untied, and her gown was in danger of slipping off her shoulders.

Rudolf's fingers itched to help, though whether to help her out of her gown or touch her breasts as he retied the laces for her, he wasn't sure. He knew now why he'd accepted the questionable honour of a crown. "I did it for you," he said simply. "As long as the Southern Isles are your home, this is where I shall be."

She frowned. "What will the Viken king say?"

"We will find out soon enough. His men sail home on the morrow, and they will tell him all." He waved away her worries. "I have no doubt Reidar wants to see me bend the knee with a crown on my head, so that he may laugh at me. But if he sees you, he will understand." Rudolf seized the crown and dropped it on top of a nearby chest. "Now I know how heavy the thing is, I remember why I never wanted one."

A tear slipped down Portia's cheek. "I don't understand."

Rudolf reached out to wipe it away. He never wanted to see her cry, much less make her do so. "My cousin, King Reidar, gave me leave to take a force across the sea to free the Southern Isles from Donald and his minions because I begged him to. I came for you, Portia. I took the Isles because they are your birthright, and your home, and I will not see anyone take them from you. Everything I have ever done is for you."

More tears fell, but this time Portia wiped them away herself. "Truly?"

"Truly."

She took a deep breath. "Then it is only fitting that I should do something for you, too. You must have an heir, and though it pains me to do it, I must give you one." Off slid the gown, with no help from Rudolf, puddling on the stones at her feet. She stepped out of it like a nymph out of a lake, lifting the hem of her shift.

Rudolf's breath caught in his throat as the filmy linen rose over her head before descending to join its fellow on the floor. "God, you're beautiful," he said hoarsely.

She toed off her stockings as she made her way to the bed. Naked as the day she was born, Portia spread her body across the covers, the greatest gift any woman ever gave a man.

"Please make haste, Dolf. It's cold, and I would prefer to get the painful part over with as quickly as possible." She shuddered, her nipples hardening until Rudolf could look at nothing else. "The pain was hard enough to bear the first time we did this."

Rudolf's brow furrowed. "But I thought it only hurt for a girl's first time. After that, there shouldn't be any pain." He'd never asked a girl about it, but he would never forget that first night Reidar spent with his queen. Her screams hadn't sounded pained.

"Are you sure? My sisters said their first few nights with their husbands were just as painful. It took them a full week before the act became bearable."

Rudolf had no idea – he had no experience with virgins. "You bled that first night. It takes time for a wound to heal, and perhaps that's why it took your sisters a week. It has been a week since we…since I…"

Portia wet her lips. "Can you check for a wound?" She parted her thighs wider.

Rudolf swallowed. He wanted nothing more to be inside her, loving her like Reidar did his queen. But if it meant hurting her… "Of course, I will check." He climbed onto the bed and knelt between her legs. He lifted his gaze to caress the soft skin of her inner thighs, remembering how glorious it had felt to plunge between them. Sliding between those wet lips, gleaming so tantalisingly before him now. Perfect, unbroken skin, with no wound to be seen. He wanted to reach out and stroke her, but he restrained himself. "You look perfect to me."

Portia rose onto her elbows, still frowning. "Did you check inside? It wasn't until you were inside me that I started hurting."

He lifted her legs over his shoulders, parting her lower lips with his fingers. Silky soft and so wet…his manhood grew rigid, but Rudolf fought to ignore it. Still he could not see anything but perfection. "I can't see inside you," he admitted. "But perhaps I can feel for it." He pushed a finger inside her slowly, stroking her inner walls.

She shuddered and clenched around his finger. "Dolf!"

"Did I hurt you?" He repeated the motion, more slowly this time.

She gasped. "No. You didn't hurt me. That feels…delightful."

The more he stroked, the hotter and wetter she became, until she cried out and clenched down hard on his finger as though she would keep it inside her forever.

"More," she sighed.

More...what? Rudolf slid a second finger into her, and started stroking harder. Watching her face this time, as her breathing grew shallow and her eyes closed, he sent her to her climax faster this time. God, what he would give to join her in reaching such a pleasurable peak together, he thought as she arched her back up off the bed and cried his name.

More than anything, he wanted to put more than his fingers inside her.

It would be different this time, he promised himself as he shucked off his clothes. At the slightest sign that he was hurting her, he'd stop, but he needed to be inside her. Now.

He lifted his manhood, poised to thrust deep into her.

"What are you doing?" she asked, fear darkening her eyes.

God help him, he couldn't. Couldn't hurt her again. It would kill him to see her cry and know he'd caused it.

Rudolf rolled onto his back so he lay on the

bed beside her. He ached to impale her. Soon, he promised himself.

"Just like the night we were wed," he said breathlessly. "You sit on top of me, so you can control how deep I go. There is no wound I can feel, inside or out. I won't hurt you, Portia, and this will feel better than my fingers, I promise." He prayed that this last part wouldn't be a lie. He'd never forgive himself.

"If you are sure…" Portia rose up onto her knees and shuffled until she straddled him, one leg on either side of his. "I'm afraid," she admitted.

"Don't be," he said, grabbing his cock in one hand as he rested his other hand on her hip. Gently, he guided the tip of his cock inside her, holding firmly to her hip when she reflexively flinched away. "Now, move down, Portia."

She bit her lip, nodded once, then lowered herself onto him. Inch by inch, he glided into her molten core. God, this woman was heaven. This time, he kept his eyes firmly on her face, alert for any sign of pain. He would not hurt her again while he was lost in his own pleasure.

Her mouth dropped open and her eyes widened, but still she descended, engulfing him so completely that her well-rounded backside rested against his balls.

"It doesn't hurt," she breathed. With agonising slowness, she rose up, and then down his length again. "That feels...good." She raised herself again.

If he left this all up to Portia, her next climax would take all night, so Rudolf took control. He fastened both hands around her hips and met her downward slide with a hard thrust.

She gasped, surprised, but then she smiled. "Again."

With Rudolf's help, she soon rode him in a rocking rhythm that felt every bit as good as he'd imagined it would. And when he felt her clenching around him in her third climax, Rudolf shouted her name as he found his own release.

"I love you, Portia," he gasped out, staring up at her.

Her breasts heaved as she fought to catch her breath, huffing and puffing as though she intended to blow the very castle down around them, but her brilliant smile was telling enough until she managed to say, "I love you, too, Dolf. Can we do that again?"

"Every night," Rudolf promised. "A good husband keeps his wife happy, and I intend to see you happy ever after."

She smiled mischieviously. "The tomorrow you shall take me for a ride, just the two of us, and when we reach a good place to stop, we shall make love all over again."

He stroked her leg, feeling his spirits rising once more. Portia was the only woman for him, now and forever. "Who said we must wait until tomorrow?"

Her eyes widened with alarm, before her expression softened to surprise, and she did some stroking of her own. "Don't make me wait, Dolf."

"Never again," he vowed, and when they came together again, it seemed the very air sang for joy.

About the Author

USA Today Bestselling author Demelza Carlton has always loved the ocean, but on her first snorkelling trip she found she was afraid of fish.

She has since swum with sea lions, sharks and sea cucumbers and stood on spray drenched cliffs over a seething sea as a seven-metre cyclonic swell surged in, shattering a shipwreck below.

Demelza now lives in Perth, Western Australia, the shark attack capital of the world.

The *Ocean's Gift* series was her first foray into fiction, followed by her suspense thriller *Nightmares* trilogy. She swears the *Mel Goes to Hell* series ambushed her on a crowded train and wouldn't leave her alone.

Want to know more? You can follow Demelza on Facebook, Twitter, YouTube or her website, Demelza Carlton's Place at:

www.demelzacarlton.com

Books by Demelza Carlton

Ocean's Gift series
Ocean's Gift (#1)
Ocean's Infiltrator (#2)
Ocean's Depths (#3)
Water and Fire

Turbulence and Triumph series
Ocean's Justice (#1)
Ocean's Trial (#2)
Ocean's Triumph (#3)
Ocean's Ride (#4)
Ocean's Cage (#5)
Ocean's Birth (#6)
How To Catch Crabs

Nightmares Trilogy
Nightmares of Caitlin Lockyer (#1)
Necessary Evil of Nathan Miller (#2)
Afterlife of Alana Miller (#3)

Mel Goes to Hell series
- Welcome to Hell (#1)
- See You in Hell (#2)
- Mel Goes to Hell (#3)
- To Hell and Back (#4)
- The Holiday From Hell (#5)
- All Hell Breaks Loose (#6)

Romance Island Resort series
- Maid for the Rock Star (#1)
- The Rock Star's Email Order Bride (#2)
- The Rock Star's Virginity (#3)
- The Rock Star and the Billionaire (#4)
- The Rock Star Wants A Wife (#5)
- The Rock Star's Wedding (#6)
- Maid for the South Pole (#7)
- Jailbird Bride (#8)

The Complex series
- Halcyon
- Fishtail

Romance a Medieval Fairytale series
Enchant: Beauty and the Beast Retold
Dance: Cinderella Retold
Fly: Goose Girl Retold
Revel: Twelve Dancing Princesses Retold
Silence: Little Mermaid Retold
Awaken: Sleeping Beauty Retold
Embellish: Brave Little Tailor Retold
Appease: Princess and the Pea Retold
Blow: Three Little Pigs Retold
Return: Hansel and Gretel Retold

CPSIA information can be obtained
at www.ICGtesting.com
Printed in the USA
LVOW13s0034300118
564540LV00017B/656/P